HOT SEAL, BLACK COFFEE

SEALs in Paradise
and
Dallas Debutantes

CYNTHIA D'ALBA

Dear Reader

Hot SEAL, Black Coffee is Book One of a collection of books which cross multiple book series, including SEALs in Paradise, Dallas Debutantes/McCool Family, and Grizzly Bitterroot Ranch. The books are connected by family ties, such as sisters, cousin, and brothers.

Each book in this crossover series can be read alone and does not require the reader to have read previous books.

The next page is a graphic of how these five books relate to each other.

Thank you for purchasing this book. I truly hope you enjoy the story,

Cynthia D'Alba

How These Books Connect

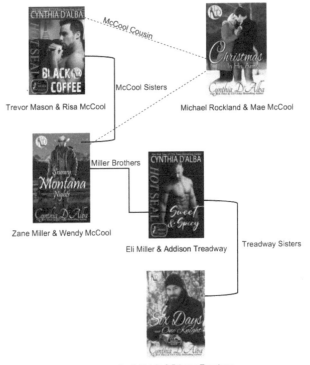

McCool Cousin

McCool Sisters

Trevor Mason & Risa McCool

Michael Rockland & Mae McCool

Miller Brothers

Zane Miller & Wendy McCool

Eli Miller & Addison Treadway

Treadway Sisters

Brody Knight & Brianna Treadway

Hot SEAL, Black Coffee

By Cynthia D'Alba

Copyright © 2018 Cynthia D'Alba and Riante, Inc.

Print ISBN: 978-1-946899-16-3

Digital ISBN: 978-1-946899-15-6

This is a work of fiction. The characters, incidents and dialogues in this book are of the author's imagination and are not to be construed as real. Any resemblance to actual events or persons, living or dead, is completely coincidental.

Cover Artist: Elle James

Editor: Delilah Devlin

To Melissa Kinnaird Wise.
Lifelong friend. College roommate. Expert Dallas Consultant.
Thank you for the ten million text message questions and phone
calls.
Any and all Dallas mistakes are mine, or total fiction that came
from my brain.

A special dedication to Dr. Issam Makhoul. Thank you for
saving my life.

Chapter One

At two-thirty Monday afternoon, Dr. Risa McCool's world shifted on its axis. He was back. She wasn't ready. But then, would she ever be ready?

Four hours passed before she was able to disengage from work and go home. As she pulled under the portico of her high-rise building and the condo valet hurried out to park her eight-year-old sedan, her stomach roiled at the realization that Trevor Mason—high school and college boyfriend and almost fiancé—would be waiting for her in her condo, or at least should be. She pressed a shaking hand to her abdomen and inhaled a deep, calming breath. It didn't work. There was still a slight quiver to her hands as she grabbed her purse and briefcase from the passenger seat.

She paused to look in the mirror. A tired brunette looked back at her. Dark circles under her eyes. Limp hair pulled into a ponytail at the back of her head. Pale lips. Paler cheeks. Not one of her better looks.

Would he be the same? Tall with sun-kissed hair and mesmerizing azure-blue eyes?

Tall, sure. That was a given.

Eye color would have to be the same, but his sun-bleached hair? His muscular physique? In high school and college, he'd played on the offense for their high school and college football teams, but she had never really understood what he did. Sometimes he ran and sometimes he hit other guys. What she remembered were strong arms and a wide chest. Would those be the same?

Almost fifteen years had passed since she'd last seen him. He hadn't come back for their tenth nor their fifteenth high school reunions. The explanation for his absences involved SEAL missions to who knew where. Risa had wondered if she'd ever see him again, whether he'd make it through all his deployments and secret ops.

Well, he had and now she had to work with him.

She took a deep breath and slid from the car.

"Good Evening, Dr. McCool," the valet said.

"Evening, John. Do you know if my guest arrived?"

"Yes, ma'am. About four hours ago."

"Do you know if the groceries were delivered?"

"Yes, ma'am. Cleaning service has also been in."

"Thank you. Have a nice evening."

"You, too."

She acknowledged the guard on duty at the desk

with a nod and continued to the private residents-only elevator that opened to a back-door entrance to her condo. After putting her key in the slot, she pressed the button for the forty-first floor and then leaned against the wall for the ride.

Her anxiety at seeing Trevor climbed as the elevator dinged past each floor. It was possible, even probable, that she had made a mistake following her mother's advice to employ his company. She was required to have a bodyguard for every public event since the announcement of the pink Breast Cancer Diamond. Her insurance company insisted on it. The jewelry designer demanded it. And worse, her mother was adamant on a guard. How did one say no to her mother?

Plus, as head of the Dallas Area Breast Cancer Research Center, she'd been tasked with wearing that gaudy necklace with a pink diamond big enough to choke a horse for the annual fundraising gala. The damn thing was worth close to fifteen or twenty million and was heavy as hell. Who'd want it?

The elevator dinged one last time and the doors slid open. She stepped into a small vestibule and let herself into her place expecting to see Trevor.

Only, she didn't.

Instead there was music—jazz to be specific. She followed the sounds of Stan Getz to her balcony, her heart in her throat.

A man sat in a recliner facing the night lights of Dallas, a highball in one hand, a cigar in the other.

"I'm glad to see you stock the good bourbon," he

said, lifting the glass, but not turning to face her. "And my brand, too. Should I be impressed?"

Her jaw clenched. Their fights had always been about money—what she had and what he didn't.

"I don't know," she said. "Are you impressed?"

He took a drag off the cigar and chased the smoke down his throat with a gulp of hundred-dollar bourbon. "Naw. You can afford it."

"Are you going to look at me or will my first conversation with you in fifteen years be with the back of your head?"

After stabbing out the cigar, he finished his drink, sat it on the tile floor, and rose. Lord, he was still as towering and overwhelming as she remembered him. At five-feet-ten-inches, Risa was tall, but Trevor's height made her feel positively petite. As he turned, every muscle in her body tensed as she stood unsure whether she was preparing to fight him, flee from him or fuck him.

"Hello, Risa."

His voice was deep and thick and smoky and she almost climaxed just hearing her name on his lips.

"Trevor. You look good." Talk about an understatement…like calling a hurricane a little wind and rain.

"Wish I could say the same." He stepped toward her. "You look…" He tucked a loose piece of hair behind her ear. "Still beautiful. Still sexy as hell, but, damn, you look tired."

She sighed. "I'm exhausted. Sorry I wasn't here to

meet you. One of my cases had a complication that kept me at the hospital until now."

He nodded. "Your office let me know." He gestured around at her condo. "Penthouse. Impressive. Cutting on folks must pay well."

She tensed and her eyes narrowed. Sure, her specialty paid well. A reward for years of grueling hard work and study. But the demands of the classroom had paled in comparison to the impossible hours of her surgery residency and breast cancer fellowship. There had been weeks when she'd barely seen her tiny apartment

When Risa had finished her fellowship and taken a position with Dallas Area Breast Cancer Research Center, she's spent the first few months driving between Diamond Lakes and Dallas. The drive, while not arduous, was long and, after too many twelve-hour days, something she began to loathe. As a birthday surprise, her parents bought the penthouse floor for Risa and her twin, Wendy, in a new high-rise being constructed in downtown Dallas. Each residence took up half the floor, so she and Wendy were they only occupants.

For Risa, the building was a little over the top. Fancy. Shiny. Exclusive.

At first, she'd been uncomfortable with all the amenities, like the twenty-four hour concierge desk, valet parking and exclusive residents-only private elevators. However, since she become head of the center, there were many nights when she arrived home after fourteen-hour days exhausted to her core. After the first few times when she'd handed over her car to be valet parked, then dragged herself to her condo to find that her groceries had been purchased and put away, she'd decided maybe this wasn't so bad after all. Sure, the monthly fees were steep, but she owned the condo outright, so no monthly note. Besides, she could afford it.

For Wendy, their parents couldn't have hit a longer homerun. Fancy, shiny and exclusive could be adjectives used to describe Risa's sister. She'd settled into the new place like a prized bull in a pasture with a harem of lusty cows.

So, maybe she could let his comment about her home pass, but she resented Trevor's flip remark about her life's work.

"Yeah, cuttin' on folks is just dandy," she replied with a taut jaw.

Asshole. Why had she thought this was a good idea?

He picked up his glass and gestured. "I'm pouring me another. You want one?"

"I thought you were more of a black coffee drinker."

"When I'm on the job, but off the clock, this is my drink of choice. Joining me?"

"Fine. Pour me a glass of wine. I think I have an open bottle in the refrigerator."

She feared she needed an entire bottle of wine to get through tonight. Her stomach had fallen to her knees the second she'd stared into his deep blue eyes. Eyes that had haunted her dreams for years. But tonight, the sparkle she'd seen so many times was gone. There was nothing in his gaze that told her anything about how he felt about being here, about seeing her again.

She followed him back to her wet bar, swearing to herself that she wouldn't stare at his ass, except of course, she ogled his tight butt in a pair of jeans that cupped everything—and she meant *everything*—just right.

He made himself at home behind her bar, splashing the expensive bourbon into the glass as though it was tap water. Reaching into the bar's built-in wine cooler, he pulled out an open bottle of white wine.

"This one?"

She nodded.

He poured and handed her a glass.

"Made yourself at home, I see," she drawled.

He turned around, leaned on the mahogany bar, and crossed his ankles. "Got a look at the layout." He smiled. "Your panty drawer was very well organized."

She rolled her eyes.

"I've checked out the building before I came. I met with the building's head of security when I got here." He shrugged. "I don't know why I'm here."

She gave a derisive snort. "I thought you were a bodyguard. Have I been misinformed?"

"Nope. That's what I do, but why am I *here*?" He pointed around the room with the highball glass. "In your condo? Why not put me in a hotel like all the others who are working this event? This is Fort Knox disguised as a condo building."

7

She narrowed her eyes, then gave him a stiff smile. "Tomorrow, I'm getting my grandmother's jewels from the vault and they'll be here until I can return them on Monday after the gala. Between now and the event, I have six event-related appearances. At first the plan was that I would be wearing the Breast Cancer Diamond necklace at each one. However, the designer doesn't want to reveal the necklace until the night of the gala. You know, build up the suspense, so I'll be teasing the reporters by wearing some of my grandmother's jewelry, which in itself is worth a couple of million or so. Since I don't usually keep a few million in diamonds in my home, and frankly it makes me a little nervous to do so with the whole world knowing about them, I thought it would be wiser to have someone here instead of having my bodyguard sleeping a few miles away."

"Okay." He nodded. "Makes sense." He pulled out his cell phone and tapped on the screen.

"I'll want you to escort me to the vault and back tomorrow."

He looked up at her. "Do you know what time?"

She arched an eyebrow. "Why? You have a date you have to work around?"

"My team from EyeSpy has a meeting with the Dallas police and the hotel security to review the overall security plan for the event."

"Fine." She pulled her cellphone from her pocket. "Can you put your phone number in here so I can reach you if I need to?"

He entered his phone number without comment.

His phone buzzed. "There. I have your cell number in my phone, along with your home and office numbers."

The idea that he had programmed her into his phone made her gooey inside, even as she told herself it only meant he was doing his job, not getting ready to ask her on a date.

"What time is the security meeting? I'd like to put it on my calendar."

"Eight a.m. Why? You don't need to be there."

"Since I'm this year's gala chairwoman, I should be on top of all things related to the event."

He sighed. "Don't you have to work or something tomorrow?"

"Nope. I'm off until Wednesday. I'm only working one day this week." She smiled and took a long drink of wine, something she didn't get to do very often.

"You have a lot of long weekends then?" he said, his tone a tad snarky.

Long weekends? She could barely remember the last time she'd had two days in a row off, much less four. But this event was her baby. The money raised would go a long way in funding more research for breast cancer diagnosis and treatment.

"Oh yes," she replied, putting as much sarcasm in her voice as she could manage. "I only, what did you call it? Cut folks? Right, so I only cut folks three days a week." She rolled her eyes. "I guess you had many long, relaxing weekends while you were a SEAL."

"How did you know I was a SEAL?"

She shrugged. "Grapevine."

He grunted. "Mom-vine is probably more accurate. And no, I didn't get long weekends."

"Fill my glass, and let's go to the sun room. I need to get off my feet."

He poured and then followed her to the spacious glass room that was bookended by two terraces, all of it overlooking the Dallas skyline. She dropped onto the couch and pulled off her shoes.

"Feet hurt?" he asked as he sat across from her, a modern, glass coffee table separating them.

"Feet, legs, back, shoulders. You name it, it aches," she said with a roll of her shoulders and head. Her neck popped a couple of times. "Was on my feet all day. I did six surgeries. Five of them were textbook, but..." She shrugged. "There's always going to be one case that doesn't go right, no matter what." She rested her head on the back of the sofa and shut her eyes. "Know what I mean?"

"Yeah, I know. Best laid plans and all that."

His voice had deepened, hoarsened. She opened her eyes. "Damn. I forgot about dinner. Have you eaten?"

"No. Wasn't sure what your plans were for me."

"I'm sorry. Sometimes I'm so tired when I get home, I forget to eat." She struggled to stand.

"I can take care of myself," he protested. "I'm thirty-five. I know how to fix my own dinner."

She waved at him with the glass in her hand. "Help yourself to whatever's in there."

Trevor had thoroughly explored the condo when he'd arrived, not out of nosy curiosity but for safety concerns. And no, he hadn't looked in her underwear drawer. Not that he didn't want to because holy hell, he wanted to know if she still wore thongs, but this was a job and he was supposed to be a professional.

Still, the temptation to look into every corner of her life had been there.

In the kitchen he found a note on the counter that was signed *Dominick, Home Manager*. He didn't know what a home manager was, or exactly what the job entailed. However, he had left a Caesar salad, fresh garlic bread and a baked lasagna in the refrigerator. Microwave instructions were taped to the aluminum foil covering the lasagna.

Damn, he needed a home manager, he mused as he placed hunks of lasagna on plates and then into the microwave. He watched the plates circle and thought about the woman in the other room. Still gorgeous, even with the exhaustion that was etched all over her face. She was too thin, and he suspected she was working too hard and not eating enough. That would be the girl he remembered. Nothing but straight A's would do. Extra credit? Yep, she'd do that, too.

After zapping the bread for a few seconds, he carried the two dinner plates back to the sun room, or rather, the" moon room" at this time of the night. He paused in the doorway.

Risa was asleep, her head still resting on the back of the couch, her right hand on the sofa holding the glass of wine, which was now empty. At some point, she'd pulled the elastic band from around her hair, and now, it was spread out behind her head.

A memory of her in his bed, her hair flowing over his stomach, replaced the vision in front of him. That'd been a long time ago…hell, a lifetime ago. They'd both been different people. He swallowed hard. There was no going back and thinking about what could have been. Life moved on, and so had they.

But he had loved her like no other woman then or since. They'd been so young, so sure they could face whatever life threw at them. How wrong they'd been.

A pang of jealousy rolled through him. Did she have a lover? A special friend with benefits? He knew there was no husband. His pre-assignment research hadn't revealed any men in her life, or at least her public life. And knowing his mother, she'd have told him if Risa had married. She'd been so disappointed when he and Risa had split.

His search of the condo had found no masculine soap, shampoo or cologne. None of the closets held men's clothing. Every surface and cupboard said Risa lived here alone.

He set the two plates on the coffee table separating the two facing sofas. He hesitated waking her, but she didn't look that comfortable with her head tilted back. Surely she'd get a crick in her neck.

And she would die if she knew she snored in front of him just then.

He sat beside her. "Risa." He touched her shoulder. "Risa, do you want to eat?"

She jerked awake and narrowly missed his nose

with her head when she straightened. "I'm sorry. I might have fallen asleep."

"Uh-huh. More like definitively fell asleep."

She yawned then slapped her hand over her opened mouth. "What is wrong with me? How rude. Sorry."

"Not a problem. I brought you something to eat."

She looked at the plates. "That's so sweet, but it's too late for me to eat dinner."

"Seriously? When did you last eat?"

Frowning, her eyes shifted up and to the right as she thought. "Um, maybe twelve hours ago."

"You're too thin." He picked up a plate. "Eat." When she opened her mouth to speak, he assumed she was going to argue with him. "Eat." He pushed the loaded plate toward her. "You're not going to make me eat alone, are you?"

She shook her head but there was a smile on her lips. "Okay. Maybe some salad." She took the plate.

"Maybe all of it."

She took a bite of the lasagna and let go a deep moan. "Damn, that is good."

Even though his brain knew the moan was due to the food, the sound echoed through him all the way in his gut. Blood mobilized and marched from his brain to his groin. He hopped up from the couch and turned his growing erection away from her. Not good. This job required he use the head on his shoulders and not the one between his legs. He had to get himself under control because the last thing he was going to do was let someone else—*anyone* else—protect Risa.

"Forgot something to drink. Want me to get your wine for you?"

"Water. I need a large glass of water." She set her plate on the table in preparation to rise.

He held out a hand, stopping her.

"I'll get it." And going to the kitchen would give him time to get his lust under control.

She leaned back. "This is my house. I should be waiting on you."

"I'll add it to my bill as services rendered."

RISA PULLED THE OVERHEAD BAR DOWN AND SLOWLY released it on a ten-count.

"Ten," she counted.

As she pulled down again, the door to the gym opened and Trevor walked in. She almost dropped the weights in surprise. Whoa. Dressed in a gray T-shirt with ripped-off sleeves, gray shorts, and carrying a black gym bag, he was devastating. She held her breath—which was a bad thing—as she reset the heavy weights. He looked sexy in his ratty gym clothes and morning beard. She released the overhead bar and rubbed her glove-covered hands on her thighs to soothe the itch to scratch her palms on his cheeks.

"Good morning," she said.

"You should have woken me."

His morning voice was thick and a little rough. She could only imagine what that would sound like in her ear, not that she had any plans to find out what it would really be like.

With a shrug, she said, "Why? You were dead to the world when I looked in, so I let you sleep."

"Do you always get up at five to work out?"

"No. Some mornings I get up about four-thirty."

"The military would have loved you."

She laughed.

"You don't need to lose any more weight," he admonished.

"I know, but I'm not here for that." She flexed her right arm to pop up her bicep. "I'm trying to build more muscle."

He nodded. "Mind if I join you?"

"Of course not."

He headed toward the treadmill, and she had to forcibly make herself pull her gaze off his legs. Man, he had great legs.

Leaning over for a better look, she frowned. "What happened to your thigh?"

A bandage covered about two inches on his upper, outer thigh area.

"Knife," he said without pausing

She wiped her face with the towel she'd hung over the machine. "Do I need to take a look at it?"

"Nope."

"Was it deep?"

"Yep."

"Stitches?"

"Ten."

He stepped onto the treadmill and pushed the start button.

"Let me look at it." She walked over to the treadmill and stood.

The treadmill belt sped up as he picked up his jogging pace.

"It's fine," he answered, his voice steady.

"So you get into knife fights now?" She narrowed her eyes. "Does your mother know you play with knives?"

He laughed. "She probably knows. Now, go do your own workout and leave me to mine."

"I'm going to want to have a look at the wound when you finish."

"Risa. Let it go," he said with a long sigh. "It's just a wound. It'll heal."

Stubborn man.

"Hmm." She placed her hands on her hips. "I thought I saw a slight limp last night, but decided it had been my imagination. It wasn't, was it? You're still having pain from that wound."

"I can do my job, if that's what you're worried about."

She huffed. "No. I'm a doctor. Of course I worry about people who have knife stabbings."

He looked at her with a wide grin. The effect was dazzling, almost blinding. Her stomach flopped over like a fish out of water.

"See a lot of stabbings in your line of work, do you?"

"I've seen a ton," she lied. "One more won't bother me."

"I'm sure. Now, let me finish my warm up."

She finished her weights before he did, but he quit to go up with her.

"You could have finished," she chided. "I've been riding up to my condo by myself for a while."

"Not with me as your bodyguard you haven't. How long will it take to get to our meeting this morning?"

"We should leave here by seven-fifteen."

"We'll take my car."

"Are you always this bossy?"

"Yelp."

The elevator opened and they stepped out. He pushed her behind him. From his gym bag he pulled a handgun.

"What's wrong?"

"Shh. Your door is open."

She leaned around him and he elbowed her back. Her heart raced and her muscles twitched.

"Maybe you forgot to shut it when you left this morning," she whispered. She crossed her fingers that was what had happened. Was it possible someone thought she already had all the diamond jewelry at her place? After all, the original plan had been to have the jewelry delivered to her house last week, but she'd had to alter that when another surgery had been added to her schedule.

He cocked an eyebrow. "No. I didn't. You stay here. Let me go check it out."

The door opened quietly. Trevor moved into her living room without making a sound. For a huge guy, he moved like a ghost. She clutched her hands together in a failed attempt to steady them.

From her apartment, she heard Trevor yell, "Freeze. Don't move a fucking inch."

That was followed by a loud, female scream.

Chapter Two

R isa ran through the condo until she got to her kitchen. She was the one who froze at the scene in front of her.

Vanilla yogurt dripped off Trevor's chin onto his sweaty T-shirt. Wendy's arms clung around his neck for support as she laughed. Her sister's long blonde hair was spread over Trevor's chest and shoulder. His arms wrapped Wendy's waist, his gun hanging over her ass. The grin on his face made Risa want to slap him—no, both of them.

"You scared the shit out of me," Risa said, her gaze narrowed on her sister. "What are you doing here?"

Wendy held on to Trevor, continuing to laugh. "Sorry," she finally said. "I didn't have anything for breakfast and I knew you'd had groceries delivered yesterday." She ran her tongue up Trevor's cheek to lick off the dripping yogurt. "Never tasted better."

Trevor laughed, the deep sound flipping Risa's heart.

"Never been a plate before," he joked.

"Bullshit," Wendy replied, her face lit with her megawatt grin. "I bet more than one girl has licked something on you before."

His responding chuckle sent flares through Risa. Jealousy? Anger? She couldn't put her finger on the emotion; she only knew she didn't like it.

"If you've had breakfast, Wendy, Trevor and I need to get ready for a meeting."

Wendy licked yogurt from Trevor's lip. "Yum. Guess that'll hold me until lunch."

Risa rolled her eyes. "Wendy. Let him go."

"Wow, bossy much?" She kissed Trevor's cheek and unwound her arms. "That was the best breakfast I've had in a long time."

He chuckled again and Risa fumed.

"You know, Wendy, he's here for a job, not to be your entertainment."

Wendy rolled her eyes. "Wow. Five minutes older and she thinks she's the boss of me." She looked at Trevor. "Tell me you'll have time to see me before you leave. It's been too long."

"Yeah," he said. "That'd be great."

"Have a good day off, sis," she said to Risa.

Risa scoffed. "The entire day will be consumed with annoying minutia about the gala. It's not like I'll be lounging around eating grapes."

"Whatever. See ya, Trev."

"You bet, Wendy. Hey, you'll be at the gala too, right?"

"Yep, but I won't be wearing the Breast Cancer Diamond like my sister. I'll be plain in my grandmother's diamond necklace and ring." Dramatically, she jutted out her lower lip. "Poor, poor Wendy."

"Jesus, Wendy." Risa shook her head. "Get out of here."

Wendy blew kisses and left. Her sister had always been the lively one, the life of the party. When she left a room, it was as if someone had turned off a light. This morning was no different. The kitchen was duller, dimmer without her in it. No wonder Trevor had agreed to see her before he left. Who wouldn't be attracted to her sister?

She turned to leave, but Trevor grabbed her wrist. "I'm sorry I scared you, but you did exactly the right thing."

Raising her gaze, she stared into his hypnotizing eyes. "What? Stand here while you flirted with my sister and made a date?"

His mouth gaped. "What? No. Of course not. She's your sister. I had to be nice."

She scoffed. "Thank goodness being 'nice' didn't include offering her other places on your body to lick." She jerked away. "I need to get a shower."

Why couldn't she be more like Wendy? Funny and carefree. Sexy and alluring. She didn't really blame Trevor for being a dog after a steak.

While she would never admit it, she took a little extra care with her hair and makeup, not for Trevor, but because she was the head of the committee for a very important event.

Once she was dressed in a pair of linen pants and a light-weight sleeveless top and sweater, she went looking for Trevor. She found him standing in her sunroom, looking out over the tall buildings of Dallas. He wore a pair of black jeans and a black T-shirt that stretched tightly over his broad shoulders but was loose at his waist. Over that was a light windbreaker. His feet were clad in a pair of black sneakers. Everything about him screamed bodyguard, exactly what she didn't want.

"Quite a view," he said.

"I know. There are lots of things I love about this place, but this room ranks pretty high."

He frowned. "Why are you staring at me like that?"

She sighed. "The only way you could look more like a bodyguard is if your windbreaker had *bodyguard* printed across the back in big, white letters."

He looked down at his clothes and when he raised his head, a smile twitched at the corners of his mouth. "Yeah. This is one of my 'go to' outfits. Want me to change?"

"We don't have time. Dallas traffic is going to be a nightmare as it is. I've already called down for my car, so we have to go."

"Well, call back down and tell them to forget it. I told you we're taking my ride."

"What difference does it make?"

His jaw firmed. "We're taking my car."

She bristled at his bossy tone but let him have his way.

Fine. Let him burn his gas. She didn't care.

On the ride down, he asked, "So, if I'm not your bodyguard, I guess we need to talk about how you want me to act. Boyfriend? Lover? Distant friend? *Cousin?*"

"Cousin?" She laughed. "You still haven't forgiven me for that college sorority joke, have you?"

"Nope. You know what they say…revenge is best served cold."

Chuckling, she said, "I think attentive is the right approach. Like a date or something. Can you do that?"

That's what she said, but her mind was screaming *lover!*

Wrap your arms around me. Throw your arm over my shoulder and pull me tight. Make every other female die with jealousy.

As though he'd heard her thoughts, he put his arm over her shoulder as the elevator doors slid open. "I can do that." Leaning over, he whispered, "Don't put your arm around my waist. You'll block access to my gun."

Her eyes widened and she looked up at him. "Seriously?"

With a grin sexy enough to melt panties, he said, "Seriously," and pressed a kiss to her temple. "Valet's watching," he whispered.

Her eight-year-old Volvo sat in the building's drive

with the valet standing in the driver's door. And yes, the man's gaze was glued to them.

"Of course he's watching," she said, a forced smile on her face. "He's never seen a man come out of my condo in the morning. He probably thought I was gay."

Chuckling, Trevor kissed her hair again. "Good."

She didn't know what he meant by that, but if he kept kissing her, she was going to start turning her head to intercept his lips with her own.

And she knew that was a bad idea.

The valet took her car back to the parking garage while they climbed into Trevor's black—*of course it was black!*—SUV.

"Nice." She rubbed her fingers over the interior black leather.

"It's safe, and that's what's important."

The final meeting with all the various factions of event security lasted a couple of hours. Risa was pleased that all contingencies appeared to have been covered. There'd be cops and hotel security in uniform and undercover. All of the EyeSpy team would be undercover, either as wait staff or in the crowd as attendees. While she'd met a number of times with the police and hotel security, this was the first time she'd laid eyes on the extra muscle from Trevor's company. After comparing Trevor to the other guys, she felt quite smug. She'd had the foresight to hire the best-looking man in the room, not that she'd intended to, but she was happy with how it had worked out.

Handsome. Chiseled cheeks. Tight butt. Panty-melting smile.

"Don't you agree, Risa?" the head of hotel security said.

Damn. She'd let her attention drift for a just a second.

"I'm sorry. I was thinking about…a patient. Can you say that again?"

The older man smiled. "I said I feel like the additional security is very welcome."

"Oh, yes. Me, too." She glanced around the room. "Have we covered everything?"

With that, the meeting recessed. She and Trevor headed to his SUV.

"Where to?" Trevor asked.

"We have some appointments."

"*We* do?"

"Don't worry. None of them involve pain, torture or knives."

There was something about the beatific smile on Risa's face and the twinkle in her eye that set alarms clanging in Trevor's head. Had he learned nothing from his SEAL days? Had he not learned to trust his own instincts?

Risa provided the driving directions until he turned into the Bliss Day Spa parking lot and stopped. "We're here," she announced, as though he would have any idea what she was talking about.

"Okay," he said slowly.

"We have appointments. Let's go."

She hopped from the car before he could get his

seat belt unclicked. He climbed out and had to hurry to catch her before she reached the front door.

"Wait a minute, little missy," he said, pulling her to a stop with a hold on her elbow. "What do you mean by *we*? I hope you have a mouse in your pocket, because I am not going into a day spa. No way. No how."

"Now, honey," she cooed for the benefit of the two women walking up behind them. "We talked about this."

"No, *honey*," he said with a tense jaw. "I don't believe we did."

"Y'all going in?" a heavy-set blonde drawled as she held the door open.

"Yes, we are. Thank you."

Risa pulled an extremely reluctant Trevor through the glass door. Somewhere in the back, a chime sounded.

"Welcome to Bliss," a young woman chirped from the desk. Her name tag read "Maggie." "Welcome back, Dr. McCool."

"Hi, Maggie. This is Trevor Mason. We have appointments for manicures, pedicures, and facials."

"No, *Maggie*. That's incorrect," Trevor said. "*She* has appointments for those things. I'll just, um, wait in the car."

Maggie chuckled. "First time, huh? You'll enjoy it. I promise. Sue," she called out, "put this gentleman in chair six by the other gentleman." She pointed toward the back of the room.

Trevor was shocked to see three other men with

their feet soaking in swirling tubs of water. God help him if his SEAL buds or any of his employees found out about this.

"Have a seat in the chair," the woman said. "Take off your shoes and put your feet in the water." As she was talking, the nail tech filled a tub at the base of the chair with water.

He removed his shoes and socks, pulled his jeans up to his knees and put his feet in the hot water. Sue squirted something blue in the tub and suds formed around his feet.

He had faced gunfire, knives, potential bombs, even cutthroat kidnappers, but this was scarier than all those. A woman had him barefoot with sharp instruments at her ready.

"Relax," the guy beside him said. "This isn't going to kill you."

Trevor's head snapped toward chair five. "Doesn't it embarrass you to get pedicures?"

The man grinned and leaned forward to speak in a whisper. "I'm married to a big time movie star who's on location here in Texas. I suspect none of her co-stars have rough feet and long nails. Gotta keep up my game."

Trevor nodded because he couldn't think of anything to say. Sue, his pedicure specialist, tapped on his right leg. When he looked down, she gestured for him to place his right foot on the towel-draped pedestal.

And that's when the POW torture began. It was Hell Week all over again.

She clipped, filed, and dug under every nail, clicking her tongue at his ingrown toenail as she freed the nail corner from its skin entrapment. He'd had root canals that'd hurt less than digging out that toenail.

She slapped his left leg and started the torment on his left foot, which, luckily, didn't require freeing a trapped nail. Then she slathered his feet with something gritty, like she was rubbing sand into his flesh. After she washed that off, she smeared floral scented lotion on his feet and up his legs and began a massage on his calves, insoles and toes.

He might have moaned.

Trevor moved to a manicure table when ordered, catching Risa's smile as he passed her. "Next time, I get to plan our activities."

She laughed.

The manicure wasn't horrible, but it also wasn't anything he'd put on his to-do list either. His mom wouldn't miss her manicure unless she was on her deathbed. But honestly? He just didn't get the allure.

His manicurist frowned through his entire clip, file and buff session. At the end, she put a glob of smelly lotion on his hands and began rubbing his fingers and palms and up his arms to his elbows.

"Loosen up," the manicurist ordered as she shook his left arm. "You're too tense."

Trevor bared his teeth in a smile, but he learned manicurists didn't intimidate easily. She smiled back and rubbed harder.

He finished before Risa as he declined clear nail

polish. Beside him, Risa snickered as her nails were painted with a bright red.

"But Trevor," she said, wiggling her fingers at him. "If you got red, we could match."

"Not happening," he growled, which made her laugh harder.

He also declined a facial while he waited for Risa to finish. He didn't know what a facial was and figured he didn't want to know. Besides, he liked his face the way it was.

Thirty minutes passed before Risa reappeared in the waiting area. Her face was stripped of any makeup and glowed with a dewy sheen. Man, his SEAL team would never stop laughing if they heard him use the phrase *dewy sheen.*

Risa handed two one-hundred dollar bills to the receptionist. "See you next week, Maggie."

"Have a good week, Dr. McCool."

Trevor held the door open. "You do this every week?"

"My fingernails, yes. Wasn't it fabulous?"

He threw an arm around her neck and pulled her close. "You've heard about SEAL Hell Week? Well, today made me have some serious flashbacks."

She laughed and bumped her hip on his. "Yes, but did you get a leg massage at the end of Hell Week?"

"I did not."

"See? This is so much better."

Her laughter filled an empty spot in his chest he hadn't realized he had. When she smiled, his heart almost exploded. After all these years apart with no contact, could it be possible that his feelings for her had always remained? Dormant but stirred back to life like a blow on an ember?

For lunch, they headed over to Bistro 31 because, as Risa explained, it was *the* place for lunch in the area. Lots of hob-knobbing potential. He'd laughed because he knew how much she hated that sort of thing. She must had thrown herself into the gala chairperson role with the same determination he'd seen when she'd faced any challenge. He'd learned long ago to not get between Risa and a set goal.

The restaurant offered indoor and outdoor dining. As much as he would have enjoyed sitting in an open area, he insisted on the inside for safety. Risa had huffed but not argued. The hostess found them a quiet booth near the bar. Over Risa's objections that she wouldn't be able to see who was there, he took the seat facing the room with his back to the wall.

Over a long lunch of steak for him and a seared ahi tuna salad for her, they ignored the gala and all the security and diamond details. Instead they revisited memories from their childhood, of jokes played on family and friends, football games and teachers. He noticed, and suspected she did also, that they touched every subject except them and their past relationship. What they'd felt for each other. The times they'd fallen into bed with a combination of lust and love. The painful separation that had come when she continued school at the University of Texas and he joined the Navy.

They'd tried the long distance thing. It hadn't

worked, not because they didn't love each other, but they'd both been pulled into the individual worlds they had chosen. Or at least that had been the reason they'd agreed on when they'd broken up. She was too busy with school, and he was going all over the world.

He'd left the SEALs a couple of years ago and set up EyeSpy International, a security and protection agency he'd built in Coronado, California. Three months ago, his family had had a health scare with his dad and he'd made the decision to move the head-quarters to Diamond Lakes, leaving only a satellite office out west. A lot of his team came with him. Few of his office staff did, so he'd been hiring staff since his arrival.

As he studied Risa, he couldn't help but smile. She didn't just talk. She gestured with her hands. Rolled her eyes. Moved her head side to side. So much animation. He'd missed her. He would've contacted her once his office and move got settled, or that's what his plan had been, but she'd beat him to the punch with the job.

On the other hand, she'd ripped out his heart and stomped on it, figuratively. He trusted his SEAL team. He trusted the men and women he'd hired at EyeSpy, but trusting her again with his heart? Yeah, he didn't think that was possible.

So for now, he'd protect her, enjoy being around her, and then go back to the solitary life he'd perfected.

Chapter Three

She studied him across the table—the lines etched near his eyes, the parenthesis that bracketed his lips when he smiled, the way his eyes laughed when he did—and she wondered if she—they? *him*?—should have tried harder. Usually hindsight was twenty-twenty, but not in this case. If they'd stayed together, would she have even attempted medical school? Would he have become a SEAL? Would they have resented each other for what they would've had to give up to be together?

Would they still be together?

"Hey. Where'd you go?" he asked, touching the hand she'd laid on the table.

Startled, she jerked back her hand. "What? Sorry. I was thinking about the upcoming interviews and appearances I have to do before the gala next Saturday."

"Nervous?" He sipped from his coffee cup.

"Yes and no. I mean, I've been in front of cameras

and done a ton of interviews, but those were always about my work."

"Which you are comfortable talking about," he interjected.

"Right. Now all these reporters want to talk about a fancy event and a big, honkin' diamond instead. We're asking people to pay a premium price to attend and I want everything to go without a hitch. It's important the gala is a success."

"And you're worried it won't be? After everything I heard this morning, it sounds like you've been putting all the details in place for over a year."

"I know, I know," she said with a smile. "I'm still trying to control everything."

He smiled. "If you didn't, you wouldn't be Risa McCool."

After lunch, which she insisted on paying for, they headed to the main branch of Texas Bank and Trust to collect her grandmother's jewelry. After going through all the appropriate identification and signatures, she and Trevor were left alone with a large, metal lockbox. She opened the lid and began sorting through the various pieces of jewelry her grandmother had collected.

Back in the early days of the Texas oil boom, her mother's grandfather, Cleve Billingham, had tapped an oil reserve while digging a new water well. The Billingham family's lives had changed from being simple ranchers to oil barons. Her grandmother had loved jewelry and had collected quite a bit during her lifetime. Risa's mother had inherited it, but immediately put it away for her children as she had no need for fancy jewelry. That hadn't been Robin and Sam's lifestyle and that wasn't how they'd raised their children, at least until they bought their twin daughters' ridiculously expensive condos.

Now, as Risa pulled out hunks of diamond jewelry, she shook her head. "Can you believe all this crap?"

"What? You don't want to wear this crown into surgery?" Trevor pulled a tiara from the box and put it on her head.

"That's a tiara," she corrected.

"So sorry. I was out that day of SEAL training."

She laughed. "You know, I suspect some of this is probably rhinestone, but who can tell the difference?" She held up a thick, fat bracelet laden with heavy, clear stones. "Take this, for example. Real or fake?"

He studied it. "I'd say real."

"Seriously?"

He laughed. "How do I know? It's kind of…" His voice drifted off as though he was rethinking what he'd been about to say.

"Gaudy? Flashy? Tacky?"

"Well, I might not have said tacky. Maybe flashy."

She laid the wide bracelet over her wrist. "Perfect for Wendy, wouldn't you say?"

"No. Perfect for you."

She shook her head. "I'm not like Wendy. She's the one with the sparkle. She can pull this off. On me, it'd look like I'm playing dress-up in my mother's things. Of course, if you think about it, I am."

"Honey, you're the one who sparkles. You may be

quieter than your sister, but in no way does she outshine you." He took her hands. "You have always had a quiet strength about you that was so powerful. Wendy? She's great. I adore your sister, but she's not you…not by a long shot."

Her heart sighed at his words. Her vision got a little blurry—not that she was crying. She swiped at her eyes.

"Darn dust and pollen."

He squeezed her hand and let go. "I know. Horrible stuff. Now, how much of this junk do we need?"

In the end, they loaded up the bigger, flashier pieces for Wendy and some smaller but sparkly bracelets and earrings for her. Trevor tossed in the tiara with, "Wendy will have to have this."

Risa remained inside the bank and let Trevor get his SUV. He pulled up at the entrance and she exited and made a beeline for the passenger door.

She patted the case in her lap. "I wonder how much money all this is worth."

"Need to buy a bigger condo?"

She saw the smile twitch at the corner of his mouth. "Well, there is a penthouse in another building that's available for only fifteen million…unfurnished."

He scoffed. "For that kind of money, they could throw in a loveseat or something."

When she laughed, it dawned on her that it'd been a while since she'd laughed this much or her heart felt so light. Maybe as long as fifteen years.

He refused to let the valet park his car, so they

pulled into the gated garage and parked in the penthouse's guest space. The residents' private elevator was only a few steps away and they rode it to the top of the building. Trevor insisted on carrying the heavy case with the jewelry, explaining that that was why he was here.

Once inside her foyer, Trevor said, "So, where do you want to stash a few million in jewelry? I thought maybe the building had a lockbox vault for the owners."

"No, but that would have been nice, wouldn't it? I was thinking you'd want to put them in your room, you know, mixed in with your underwear, so you could keep an eye on them."

When she saw the frown forming on his brow, she chuckled. "Kidding. I have a safe. We can put the case in there."

"Bolted down somehow, I hope."

"Oh much better. Built into the structure of the building."

"Really?" His eyebrows arched in surprise.

"I don't know about all the condos, but I know Wendy and I both have safes, so I assume everyone does. Mine and Wendy's are in different locations within our units. I've always wondered if the architect who designed the building moved safes around as a security feature."

"Interesting. So where is yours?"

"I thought you checked this place out. Didn't you find it? Here I thought you were some super spy guy," she joked.

He lifted his nose to look down at her. "Maybe if I'd been looking for a safe, but I wasn't."

She grinned. "I don't think you would have found it regardless. Come in to my bathroom."

He waggled his eyebrows. "Sounds kinky. What do you have in mind?"

She rolled her eyes. "Perv."

"Says you. I say kinky."

She was laughing as she led him through her bedroom and into the master bath. Thank goodness she'd taken the time to make up the bed and pick up her bathroom.

"You've really got a nice place," he said, nodding his head and looking around as they passed into the bathroom. "My apartment only looked this good when I'd been deployed for six months."

"And now that you're out?"

"Disaster zones instead of rooms."

"Remember the first time you took me to your bedroom, but I had to wait in the hall while you picked up all your dirty clothes?"

He snorted. "Yeah. But it looked pretty good after that, right?"

"Oh, lord, no. Your room was always a pig sty."

"I wish I could argue with you but…" He shrugged. "When you're right, you're right. Now, where is this safe?"

They had had a lot of sexy times in his bedroom… a lot of them. Remembering them made her stomach tightened. She pressed a palm to her abdomen.

"You okay? You look like you're in pain."

"Ate too much," she lied. "Okay, the safe."

She opened the door to the linen closet and removed the folded towels from the middle and bottom shelves. Once empty, she wiggled her hand under the wood of the next to the last shelf until she could touch the tiny button in the corner. She pressed it, and the empty shelf dropped flat against the wall and the back wall panel opened, which exposed a safe door with an electronic panel.

"Voilà! The safe."

He nodded. "Nice."

When she moved to punch in the code, he turned his back to her.

"What are you doing?" she asked.

"Even though you showed me the safe, I thought you'd like to keep the code secret."

"Seriously, Trevor? I trust you with my life, but not with my safe code? Goose." She tapped the back of his head.

She pressed the seven digit code and the door swung open. "Okay, you can turn around now."

He turned and handed her the case. The safe was small and as she had feared, the briefcase was too wide for the safe's width, so they had to unload the jewelry pieces and store them individually. Once the door was shut and the shelf back into place, Trevor handed her the towels for her to replace in the closet.

She shut the door and turned toward him, surprised to find him right next to her.

"I'm curious about something." He stepped closer.

"Okay." She dragged out the word in confusion. Hadn't they talked already about everything?

He slid his hand along her cheek until he could wrap his fingers around her neck. With a gentle pull, he brought her closer and pressed his lips to hers.

Lightning shot through her veins. She knotted her fingers in his shirt and held on because surely her knees would fail her.

The first kiss was a simple mouth on mouth touch. He pulled back and looked into her eyes. She was sure her face was flushed and her eyes begged for more.

This time, he jerked her flush against him, trapping her hands until she could pull them out and glide them up and around his neck. Her breasts flattened against his hard chest. Her bones melted in his embrace.

He flicked out his tongue and touched her lip. She opened her mouth and he slid inside, caressing her tongue and cheeks.

Pulling away, he adjusted his head and took the kiss deeper to a more sensual level. He pressed his hard cock to her groin and she moaned as she thrust against him.

He took another step forward and she stepped back until she was crushed between his granite body and her linen closet door. His hand was at her waist, but he moved it slowly up her side until his fingers rested just below her breast. Her tongue pushed into his mouth, thrilling at his taste. It felt like coming home after a long trip.

Abruptly he pulled away his mouth and stepped

back, his breathing coming in ragged pants. Her hands slid from his neck and back to her sides.

She swallowed. "Did you find out what you wanted to know?"

Before he could answer, a voice called from the foyer, "Risa? You home?"

Risa found her sister standing in the living room wearing a scarlet-red, long, form-fitting dress.

"What do you think?" Wendy asked. She held her arms out and turned in a full circle.

"Nice," Risa said.

Trevor whistled. "That's going to knock someone's eyes out. What's the event?"

"The Breast Cancer Gala." She snorted. "You already forget?" She twirled again. "So, tell me how great this dress looks on me."

Risa arched an eyebrow. "I thought you were wearing that black dress, you know, the one you bought last month."

"That was last month. I found this baby today and just had to have it." She fanned out the material in the front. "It's not too much do you think?"

"Nope," Trevor said before Risa could say a word. "You are sexy as hell in that thing."

"You look lovely," Risa said, wanting to bash Trevor over the head…and then bash her sister for, well, being Wendy mostly. She wasn't jealous over how beautiful her sister looked or how appreciative Trevor's expression was. It was that Wendy had come at an inopportune time.

Yeah, she could lie with the best of them.

"Have you been to the vault yet? What did you get for me to wear with this?" Dramatically she crossed her fingers. "Tiara?"

Risa sighed. "Yes, I brought *the* tiara."

"Yay," Wendy said and high-fived Trevor. "Did you see it, Trev?"

He smiled. "I did. Fancy."

"I know. Show me, show me," she said.

"Do you really need it right now?"

"Yes. I want to look through all of Grandma Billingham's jewelry and decide what I'm going to wear."

"Fine. Wait here and I'll go get all the jewelry."

The aroma of fresh coffee tickled her nose as Risa walked back carrying all the boxed jewelry. She found Trevor and Wendy in her kitchen, him with a mug of coffee and her sister sipping from a glass of red wine.

Make yourselves at home is what she wanted to say. But she caught herself. Wendy and she had always made themselves at home in each other's condos. This should be no different, even as a tug of jealousy jerked in her belly.

"Here it is." She held out the boxes.

"Hope you don't mind," Trevor said, gesturing with his mug.

She scoffed. "Of course not. I told you the first night to help yourself."

"See? I told you she wouldn't mind," Wendy said. "Now, let me take a look."

Trevor sipped his black coffee and studied the

twins. Other than a birthday and parentage, they shared almost nothing in common.

Risa was gorgeous, in her own quiet way, while Wendy was flamboyantly attractive.

Risa's wavy dark hair held a glowing luster. Her green eyes were perfectly shaped. And when she smiled, her whole face lit up.

Wendy's blonde hair was long and straight. Her green eyes lacked all the personality Risa's had. Her smile and personality did sparkle, but he didn't feel the pull he did with Risa.

Sure, now that he compared, their noses were similar, as were their mouths, but that could be so with any siblings. And they were both smart, as evidenced by their successful careers.

Nope. No comparison. Risa was the complete package, in his humble opinion. Wendy, while a stunning woman, was a pale imitation of her sister.

Wendy set the tiara on her head, and Risa laughed. As they continued to try on the various pieces, he sat back and thought about the kiss. The one that'd blown his socks off.

He'd wondered if the chemistry between them was still there. He'd suspected it was on his end ever since she'd said his name last night, but on her side? He hadn't been sure until about ten minutes ago. Now, he was.

Time and distance hadn't dimmed their sexual attraction at all. For him, maturity and life experiences made him realize how exceptional Risa was and how unique his feelings were for her.

He could even forgive her for breaking up with him. Looking back, he could clearly see it had been for the best, for both of them, even if she could have picked a better time than the start of Hell Week.

Sexual chemistry was one thing. They had had, and apparently still had, enough chemistry to launch rockets. However, commitment was a totally different animal. Even if he believed himself ready for a lifetime commitment—and he wasn't one-hundred percent sure he was there yet—he had no idea if he could let the past go and let her back into his closed circle. And, without a shadow of a doubt, this was not the time to discuss or even think about the future. He had to get through the week and the weekend. Only after could he then face whatever decisions had to be made.

"Thanks for picking up all the stuff." Wendy started piling up the boxes containing the jewelry.

"Um, Wendy," Risa said, "I think it'd be better if you left those here and get everything just before the party."

Wendy frowned. "Why? It'll be fine in my condo. I have a safe."

"I know, but I'm responsible for all that." She wrinkled her nose. "Make me happy. Leave it here until Saturday."

Her sister winked. "And besides, you have the hunky guard living here to protect the jewelry, right?"

Trevor grinned and saluted with his mug. "Here and on duty."

Risa gathered up the boxes to return to the safe. "What are you doing tonight? Got a date?"

"Nope. Had one with Everett Livingston, but he canceled."

"Why?"

"Something about his grandmother and dinner with the family. Doesn't matter. I'll see him tomorrow anyway. We have a double date with his little brother and our cousin." She grinned. "I think we made a love match by introducing them."

"Really? That's nice," Risa said. "Opal Mae is such a sweet girl, but Aunt Alice didn't do her any favors with that name."

Wendy rolled her eyes. "No kidding.

"Everett your date for the event?" Trevor asked.

"Yep."

"Dates two weekends in a row. Sounds serious," he joked.

"Heaven forbid," Wendy gasped dramatically, and then smiled. "Not really. Everett looks good, knows how to behave in public, never cusses, and has tons of money."

"Ah. I see. The perfect arm candy," Trevor replied.

"You know it. Don't have to see him during the week, and he shows up in time to buy me dinner on the weekend." She chuckled. "Besides, I feel responsible for Opal Mae and Roy's future. I don't want to put Opal Mae in a tough situation with the Livingston family. I worry about her though. I think she might be more serious than Roy." She waved her hand. "But who knows? What are you two doing tonight?"

Trevor looked at Risa.

She answered with a shrug. "Probably nothing. Dinner in, watch a movie maybe. That okay with you, Trev?"

"Sure. I know my digestion will be happier near the jewelry I'm supposed to be watching."

"Sounds good to me," Wendy said enthusiastically. "Let me run home and change clothes and I'll be right back. Find us a good movie, Risa."

"Super," Risa said as the door slammed behind Wendy.

"Before she comes running through the door again…" Trevor reached out and pulled Risa to him. "I had had more plans like this." He lowered his head and she met him halfway. Their mouths met in a clash of lips, teeth and tongues. His heart swelled in his chest, as his cock swelled in his jeans. She ground on him and he groaned.

"I know how to kill people so it looks like an accident," he said against her lips.

She laughed. "Tempting, but she's my sister."

He rested his forehead on hers. "Think she'll stay to the end of a movie?"

"Oh, yes."

"Think you can find something short to watch? Maybe a thirty-minute sitcom and tell her it was a movie and she slept through it?"

She snorted. "I can try. Now, let me go so I can find something for the three of us to eat."

"Nope." He slipped his arm around her shoulders. "Where you go, I go."

She gave him a sideways glance. "Well, that could get interesting."

"That's sort of what I have in mind." He pumped his eyebrows for effect, then kissed her again.

In the distance, the elevator dinged.

Trevor raised his head. "Can you please lock the door in the future?"

Risa grinned and slipped from his arms. "She has a key."

"Damn it," he said under his breath.

"Stay in here and keep her company."

Wendy breezed through the door before he answered.

"I'm going to lock up these," Risa said, pointing to the boxes of jewelry. "Then I'll see what I can find for dinner. Keep Trevor company, okay?"

"Sure. Hell, we haven't seen each other in forever," Wendy said, fluttering her eyelashes. "Hey Trev, remember the time Risa and I hid your clothes while you were skinny dipping?" She pulled Trevor down onto the sofa beside her.

Risa shook her head, gathered up the boxes, and said, "We swore we'd never tell him that was us."

Trevor laughed. "Like I didn't know."

As soon as Risa left the room, Wendy's friendly expression fell away. "What are you doing?"

He frowned. Her whispered question had been just short of anger.

"What do you mean? My job."

"Your job involves kissing my sister?"

Hell, the clueless one actually noticed? "Umm…"

"Yeah, that's what I thought. You think I wouldn't notice her mouth looked all kissed and swollen?" She punched his shoulder. "Damn you, Trevor. She almost went crazy the last time you two split. Depressed for months. Don't do this to her."

"I'm not doing anything. We kissed. So what? We're both adults."

"That's not the issue." She looked toward the door and back to him. "I beg you. You don't know what it did to her the last time. And then when you were overseas on missions? Shit. She would bury herself in books and projects, and I know she did that to keep you out of her head. Now, here you are again, all mister Nice Guy, flying in, saving the day, and flying out again." She shook her head. Her jaw was locked tight. Her lips a straight line.

He pulled in a deep breath and checked the door to make sure Risa wasn't standing there listening. "Let's get a drink." He jumped up and headed for the bar. There he grabbed the bottle of bourbon, filled a glass, and took a gulp.

"What in the hell are you doing?" Wendy asked. "Give me that booze. You're supposed to be on duty." She put air quotes around on duty. She pulled the glass from his hand and took a drink, followed by a grimace. "Ick. Where's the red wine? And why are we over here? And why do you need a drink?"

He made a face. "You give me a headache, Wendy."

She gave him a mean scowl. "I'll give you more than a headache if you hurt my sister, asshole."

"I won't." He poured her a red wine. "I promise. I'm not here to hurt her. I'd never hurt Risa."

"Not on purpose," she hissed. "But kisses and touching? And *ohmigod*, don't tell me you've slept together."

"If we had—and we haven't—that would be none of your business."

When he took a step away, Wendy grabbed his arm. "I'm serious, Trev. You hurt her and—"

"I was going to ask what you thought about pizza," Risa said from the doorway, her gaze shifting between the two of them. "Think you can let go of Trevor long enough to tell me where you want to order it from?

Wendy produced a theatrical sigh. "If you insist."

She kicked a foot up behind her and booted his ass. Then she walked into the kitchen.

"That wasn't what you think," Trevor said.

Risa held up a hand. "Doesn't matter. Don't want to talk about my sister." She followed Wendy into the kitchen.

He knew he was in trouble, but he couldn't help wondering if Risa might have been a little jealous— but of Wendy? Her own sister? How could she think he would kiss her, then turn around and also be attracted to her sister? And worse, how could she think he would be making moves on both of them?

Trevor knew tension. Hadn't he and his team felt it before every mission? The tension in the room as they waited for the pizza delivery felt as thick and heavy as a wet blanket.

Still, he had to give Wendy credit. She was the one who kept the conversation flowing by asking about his missions. He answered with as much as he could say. Then she moved on to his team. When he explained about the team, and how each guy had a different signature drink, she insisted he tell her each drink and about the man who drank it. When he got to Dirtman and his dirty martini, he then had to confess that Dirtman had landed a home renovation reality show on some obscure cable channel.

"When is it?" Risa asked, her first contribution to the discussion.

"Thursday night at seven or eight. I've forgotten. But like I said, the show is on some obscure channel."

"Which one?"

"HNS. I think that stands for the Home Nation Station."

Risa looked it up on her phone and smiled. "Got it."

"Oh, I want to watch it too." Wendy looked at him with an arched eyebrow. "Is this guy cute? Is he single?"

Trevor shook his head and laughed. "I have no idea whether he's cute. None whatsoever. Single? At last report, Dirtman is single, but your match-making brain hasn't factored in that he lives on the beach in California."

Wendy gave a careless shrug. "I can move."

Risa swatted her sister. "You cannot. Who would I work with?"

"Oh, come on, Risa. Dallas has more than its fair

share of excellent plastic surgeons. Sad to say, but I'm replaceable."

"Not to me." Risa grabbed her sister's arm. "Don't even joke about moving away."

As Trevor watched and listened to the sisters' squabble, he saw family. His SEAL team had been— and probably always would be—a type of family for him. But he missed his parents and his brother. His dad's health scare had brought him home, but in the short time he'd been back, he felt his roots settling into the dirt, and he liked the feeling. His years of service had kept him on the move with no ties to hold him down. It'd been a good life, but he was ready to move on to the next stage of his life.

If only he knew what that was.

"Remember that, Trev?" Wendy asked.

"Sorry. Zoned out for a second. What should I remember?"

"Do you remember when you and Risa broke up right after the homecoming dance during our senior year?"

He glanced at Risa, who arched a brow. He wondered exactly what they'd been talking about while he'd visited old home week in his head.

"Of course. Why?"

"Remember what you did? You asked out the cutest girl one year behind us." Wendy knocked Risa's shoulder. "You were livid."

He grunted. "Not so livid that she didn't turn down a date with what's-his-name. You know. That guy who was a brainiac like her."

"Tim McClure." Risa said, lifting her chin. "Such a gentleman."

Trevor narrowed his eyes. "Not so much of one at the end of the night when he parked at Emerald Lake and wanted to make-out."

Risa gasped. "How did you know about that?"

Trevor cleared his throat. "I may have followed you."

Wendy snorted and slapped her hand over her mouth. "You did not."

"Trevor!" Risa's eyes were wide. "You followed us?"

He lifted his hand as though taking a pledge. "Hand to God, it's true. I was about ready to pull you out of that car when the engine started and he took you home."

"Did you threaten to beat him up if he asked her out again?" Wendy asked with a sly smile.

He startled. "Who told you?"

Wendy giggled.

Risa grabbed his forearm. "You didn't."

Trevor shrugged. "Maybe."

"He never asked Risa out again and would barely speak to her," Wendy said. "Then there was the time when Mr. Barron, their chemistry teacher, assigned Tim and Risa to work together on a project. Tim met with Barron, new assignments were made and Risa had to work with Smelly Larry."

Trevor chuckled. "Smelly Larry? What are you? Ten?"

Wendy laughed. "Yeah, I know but I was awful back then."

"Back then?"

She rolled her eyes. "Fine, I'm awful today too."

"Why in the world did you go down that memory lane?" Risa frowned.

"Oh. I ran into Tim McClure last week."

"Really?" Risa said, her face brightening with a smile. "How does he look?"

Trevor lips tightened. Seriously? After Wendy's lecture about not hurting her sister, she then goes and brings up the only guy Trevor had to threaten more than once to stay away from his girlfriend? And there might have been a few shoves and punches to get his message across. Damn.

"Oh good. Really, *really* good."

"Is he back in Diamond Lakes?"

"Better. He's here in Dallas. Divorced. Said he has a couple of kids. Moved here to be closer to them."

Risa's smile widened. "Good for him. I bet he's a great dad."

"Maybe," Trevor said, his voice sour with disgust at the conversation. "But he must have been a horrible husband."

Risa turned her bright smile toward him. "Maybe it was *her* fault their marriage failed."

"Maybe it was nobody's fault," Wendy said with a shoulder bump to Risa. "Maybe he never got over the one who got away."

Trevor blew a puff of disgust. "Give me a break. That was twenty years ago and one date."

Wendy smiled sweetly. "I never said anything about him and Risa." Laughing, she stood. "Well, I've gotta go. It's getting late. Need to get my beauty sleep."

She charged through the condo and the front door slammed behind her.

"Was it something I said?" he asked.

She laughed.

"How about that movie?"

She checked her phone. "It's getting a little late."

He frowned. "It's nine o'clock. When we are fifty-five and we hesitate to start a movie at nine because it's too late, that'll be fine. But I think we can both stay up past ten. Come on. What's on?"

"Fine," she said with a whirl toward the TV in the den. "What do you want to watch?"

"Hmm…blood, gore, and violence?"

She snorted. "Nope."

After turning to the available movies, she began scrolling.

"No bloody, gory war movies. I get enough blood and gore at work."

"Fine." When she stopped at a Jane Austen movie, he groaned. "No. Please. No movies about Regency England and no gooey, love stories."

"Fine." She scrolled on until she found a sci-fi movie with lasers, bombs and a love story.

"What about this?"

"Sold. But before we get started, I want to make sure all the doors are locked," Trevor said.

"Afraid my sister will be back?"

He chuckled. "No, but checking doors and windows is why I'm here, right?"

He waited, hoping that she'd say something about reconnecting or missing him or anything that would be other than professional reasons. Sure, she'd kissed him, but he needed some words.

After hesitating a minute, she shrugged. "Right, but I can do it. I know how to lock everything. Be back in five."

"Nope. I'm with you. I want to check everything myself."

She hopped up. "Knock yourself out!"

They made the rounds to the front door—locked —then by each of the sliding doors that led out to the terrace. There must have been at least six of them, each locked with a security bar. Then she led him to the rear entrance where the residents-only elevator opened directly into her suite.

"Okay, this I don't like," he said, examining the elevator. "I mean, anyone could get on here, take this to the penthouse and enter your condo."

She shook her head. "Not really." She turned a lock on the elevator frame. "This locks the door, so it can't be opened without this key," she said, flashing a gold key. "Plus it only opens to my rear entrance where I stash my umbrella or wet shoes or whatever might be dirty." She pulled him back into the condo. "And then this door locks." She bolted a rear door. "Now that I think about it, you're probably an overkill." Looking up at him, she added, "You can thank my mother for this job. She insisted."

"I'm glad you're on the top floor of the building. It does make breaking in more challenging."

She laughed. "Seriously, Trevor? You think you could break in?"

"Probably not me, but I know a few guys who could."

"You hang around with some strange people."

He shrugged. "The job. Now, the movie, and then get some rest. I checked the schedule and we have to be at the television station early."

"Popcorn?"

"I'm stuffed from the pizza, aren't you?"

"Well, yeah, but I was trying to be a good host."

"I'm not a guest, Risa," he said softly." I'm your employee, right?"

"Right."

Her answer was a quick jab at his gut.

They settled onto the sofa, close but not touching. He put his arm along the back of the cushion and settled in to watch spaceships battle.

At the same time, the evening's conversation ran through his head. He wasn't sure what he'd expected or wanted her to say about their past, maybe that they'd been good together. And then for him to get jealous as soon as Tim McClure's name came up? He hoped she hadn't noticed.

And damn it, he wanted her to say she was glad he was here and that hadn't happened either. Maybe he shouldn't have waited fifteen years to come back to her.

Chapter Four

For years, Risa had held her emotions in check. She'd dated, but not often and rarely beyond a second date. Most of the men who were interested in her were, in her opinion, just as interested in her fancy condo with its prime Dallas location or her parents' ranch in Diamond Lakes or wanted to tap into her medical resources. She couldn't remember the last guy she'd believed was interested in Risa, the person.

She did have one good friend who would attend professional functions with her when she needed an escort, but there was nothing between them. He claimed a bisexual orientation, but she'd always felt he leaned more toward men than women and would probably be happier with a man. Still, he was reliable, handsome, and charming—the ideal date when she didn't really want a date, but to attend without one would be awkward.

Beside her, however, sat the biggest threat to her heart that she'd had in more than a decade. Like her usual escort, Trevor was handsome and charming. The stopper came at reliable. Was he? She had no clue. He'd been a rolling stone for so long that, well, a rolling stone could be difficult, if not impossible, to settle in one place. After all, hadn't he started the business in California, and then moved it to Texas? Rolling stone.

She was settled. She loved Dallas. Loved her job. Loved being close to her family. Loved having her twin just down the hall. Did she want to upset her perfect life by letting Trevor in, especially knowing he would be gone in five days?

And even if he did stay, his time would be consumed with his company. She didn't know much more than what she'd read and what his mother had told her mother, but an international security company would certainly take him out of town, and out of the country on a regular basis. Always on the move. Always rolling to a new place and new challenges.

And the people he knew…He'd been serious about knowing someone who could get through all her security, and that scared her. One of the reasons she hadn't stayed with him fifteen years ago had been because the thought of him being in harm's way paralyzed her with fear. She couldn't study. Couldn't sleep. Would only eat enough to keep herself alive.

Finally, she'd blocked him from her thoughts. It'd only taken a couple of years before he wasn't the first thing she thought of in the morning and the last thing she thought about at night. Although to be honest, she'd never really forgotten him. There had been many "what ifs" over the years.

While he probably didn't believe her story, it had been his mother, via her mother, who'd suggested hiring him for this event. Her mother told her that Mrs. Mason was so happy that Trevor had finally come back to Texas and they'd be able to see him more often.

Being a nice, middle-class family, the Masons could never have afforded the fifty-thousand per ticket for the gala, but she'd sent his parents' tickets as a thank-you for getting Trevor to take this job.

"Have you talked to your folks?"

Trevor was facing the movie, and she assumed he was engrossed because it took a minute for him to answer. He paused the action on the screen. A couple of the characters were shooting laser guns at each other.

"What?"

"Have you talked to your parents since you've been here?"

"No. When would I? We've been on the go all day."

"I don't know. I thought maybe you called them last night."

"Nope." He turned the movie back on.

"Why not?"

He sighed and stopped the action again. "I don't know. I just haven't."

She turned on the sofa to face him. "Do you want

to drive down on Sunday and see them? We have time."

"No. We need to stay here. All your family jewelry will still be here, so I need to be here."

"Hmm."

Wrapping a hand around her ankle, he pulled her down the couch until she was beside him. Once there, he snaked his arm around her shoulders until his hand was over her lips.

"There. Now I can hear the movie."

She giggled, and then, she had no idea what possessed her, but she licked his fingers.

His head jerked toward her and their gazes met. His eyes darkened and smoldered with lust.

Her heart leapt into her throat and she could barely draw a breath. His hand moved slowly away from her mouth.

"My tongue slipped?"

"Yeah? I think my tongue might slip too."

He pulled her over and kissed her…a long, deep, tongue-thrusting kiss that must have lasted thirty minutes. During that time, he gently lowered her back to the sofa and followed her down, their lips never more than a millimeter apart.

When she scooted backwards so her legs stretched out on the cushions, he wedged himself between her thighs and continued caressing her mouth, inside and out. Finally, he pulled away and left a line of kisses up her cheek and to her ear. Using the tip of his tongue, he traced her ear's outer rim and left a breathy moan whispering in her ear.

He jerked his mouth away and sat up. "This movie's not that great. Why don't you get some sleep? We have an early start tomorrow." He stood. "I want to check the terrace doors one more time before you call it a night."

She stared for a full ten seconds, and then she slapped a hand on the sofa cushion. Sleep? She'd never get to sleep with memories of his kisses rolling through like a film strip.

But she'd be damned if she let him know he'd gotten to her.

She marched to her room and slammed the door… two or three times. She had to make sure it was shut tight to keep burglars and ne'er-do-wells out of her room.

Rising before the sun wasn't an issue for Risa. She'd had ranch chores before breakfast as far back as she could remember. One sleepless night couldn't shake her. However, she was going on a second night of rolling around in her sheets like clothes in a dryer.

At four, she gave up any pretense of sleep and hopped into the shower. On surgery days, she didn't usually put on makeup or do much to her long hair other than pulling it back into a ponytail. Surgery required masks—which would smear her makeup—and a cap, which would effectively leave her to deal with flyaway hair.

This morning was different. A television appearance, newspaper interview, the keynote address at a civic club meeting, and the evening drive radio program required she polish up her exterior.

At four-forty-five, she exited her bedroom and sighed as the aroma of freshly brewed coffee wafted down the hall.

In the kitchen, Trevor stood frying bacon and sipping coffee. He'd dumped the all-black bodyguard look in favor of khaki slacks, a white oxford shirt rolled up to mid-forearm, a black, tailored jacket and soft-soled shoes.

"Good morning."

His voice was deep and made her think of dark rooms, soft sheets and a king-sized bed.

She fought the shiver that ran down her spine.

"Good morning," she repeated, her voice raspy and rough. "How long have you been up?" She cleared her throat. Her voice needed a little exercise before she had to speak on television.

"A while. Put some breakfast in your belly."

"I'll just have coffee." She poured a cup and took the plate he shoved in her hand.

"Eat. We have time."

The front door bell chimed and her head snapped up. "That's not supposed to happen. No one comes up the guest elevator without prior announcement."

"Finish eating. I know who this is."

He left the kitchen, and she followed him to the front entry way, the formal guest entry.

After looking through the peephole, he opened the door with a bright smile.

"Sue. Thank you for coming."

"Are you kidding? The job entails sitting in this

incredible condo all day? Thanks, Boss. Can I request more jobs like this?"

He chuckled and turned around. "I knew you wouldn't follow directions." He sighed. "Risa, this is Sue Lee, the fastest, meanest chick I've ever met."

"And the only one to put you on your back." She arched a brow in challenge. "And don't call me a chick."

He laughed. "One of these days, I'll demand a rematch. Sue, this is Dr. Risa McCool. This is her home. I expect today to be the most boring job ever, but we have some outside appearances and I don't want to leave her safe unguarded."

"Nice to meet you," Risa said, extending her hand.

Dressed in black, form-fitting jeans, a tank top and EyeSpy windbreaker, Sue wore the confident expression of someone who wasn't afraid of anything or anyone. Her shiny, long, black hair was pulled into a ponytail, which might have added an inch to her petite stature.

Sue shook her hand. "You too."

"Let me give you the five-cent tour," Trevor said, gesturing for Sue to follow him.

"I can show her around," Risa said. "This is my house."

"You." Trevor pointed toward the kitchen. "You, go eat. Sue won't care about your fancy carpets and Monets on the wall. She's only interested in potential ingresses and egresses."

Risa whirled around and headed back to the

kitchen, her jaw tight with fury. What did he mean by that snarky remark? Was he always going to be uncomfortable that her family was lucky enough to have some cash reserves?

It was high school all over again.

As he'd asked—or maybe ordered—that depended on whether she wanted to overlook his demanding tone—she nibbled on a piece of toast and thought about their on-again-off-again relationship. Seemed like their issues always centered around her family's money, which was so stupid. Whenever she'd bought him a gift he deemed too expensive, he'd get furious and, sometimes, refuse it. Like the time she'd secretly paid for his car to get the engine repairs and new tires it desperately needed. He couldn't exactly ask the garage to undo all their work and his car had needed tires so badly his mother had wept and hugged Risa. Trevor, however, wasn't the least bit pleased. Instead, he'd been irate, and she hadn't understood his anger. Now, looking back, she could see she should have gotten his permission before overhauling his car. Her actions might have been a little high-handed, but she'd meant well.

"Ready?"

Risa raised her gaze from her plate, where she'd been focused, to Trevor's chiseled face.

"As ready as I'll ever be. You didn't show your guest where the kitchen is."

"Sue isn't a guest. She's an employee, and yes, she's familiar with the layout. Let's get a move on if you don't want to be late."

"Your car again?"

He smiled, and her panties got wet.

Damn it.

"Never mind," she said, slinging a purse over her shoulder. "Of course, you're driving."

When she headed toward the residents' elevator, he put a hand on her shoulder to stop her. "Let's use the public elevator system. I'd rather your doors stayed locked."

"Sure. Whatever."

The ride to the KSEP studio was quiet. She wasn't really comfortable being in the spotlight, an aspect of her career that she hated. However, she much preferred being known for her work rather than for her family's last name. It wasn't as if reporters followed her on dates or tried to take pictures with long-range lens, but she and or her sister had been in the society pages since their debutante days. She'd been known for performing the perfect Texas dip, while Wendy became known for doing the splits under her ball gown instead of the tucked-legs pose. However, her sister was so well-loved that everyone laughed with Wendy, never at her. Had Risa been the one to do the splits, the outcry of pity and sympathy would have been smothering.

But her saving grace that long-ago evening and for all the fancy la-de-da events during her debutante year had been Trevor. She'd leaned on his quiet strength when she was at her most stressed. Had she ever thanked him? All those events. All those times when he'd had to wear a suit when she was sure he'd rather have been in jeans on the back of a horse.

And wasn't that exactly what she'd asked him to do again for her? Protect her. Shield her. Keep her safe. Would she always look to him as her tower of strength? What would happen when the day came— and she was positive it would—that she needed his quiet presence again to ground her, to stabilize the craziness?

"We're here. Let's go slay some dragons."

Risa laid her hand on his arm before he could slide from the car. "Did I ever thank you for being my deb escort?"

His heart jumped at her touch. His brain, however, was confused. "What? Your deb thing, like a million years ago?"

"Yeah. That. I don't know if I ever told you how much I appreciated all you did, all you had to endure. I know some of those outings were beyond boring, but you were such a good sport. You always knew how to make me relax and smile."

"Why would you bring that up now at…" he checked the time, "five-thirty in the morning?"

"I don't know. You know how my brain works. I think of one thing, that leads to another thing and another and before you know it, I'm reliving the dreaded Texas dip."

"Ah. The dip. The requirement to basically twist yourself in to a pretzel while lowering yourself to the floor in some act of degrading debasement." He laughed, so she'd believe he was kidding, but he wasn't. He'd never thought Risa should bow to anyone.

She slapped his arm playfully. "You're horrible. The Texas dip is…is…okay, well, maybe it does twist a gal around a bit. Anyway, thank you."

"My pleasure. Any time spent with you is the high-light of my day. Now, get a move on."

As soon as they entered the studio, a program assistant whisked Risa away. He didn't follow, but he didn't let her out of his sight either. That conversation in the car still baffled him. After all these years, why bring up her debutante days? He'd been incredibly relieved that she'd never known how strapped for money he'd been back then and that most of his clothes had been borrowed or bought at secondhand shops. Being around all the rich snobs—which did not include the McCool family—they were as down-to-earth as anyone could be.—had left him antsy and worried that someone would notice or comment on his clothing. No one had. It wasn't until years later that he'd realized no one had given his clothes a second glance because they'd been more concerned about how *they* looked or what others thought of them.

Now, he watched as an assistant placed a lapel mic on Risa's jacket and then trailed the wire pack down her side and around to her back. Trevor leaned against a wall and soaked in the view of the ideal woman. Calm. Collected. Completely at ease in any environment. The camera came on, and the interview began. Risa hit every question with facts and heart-stopping smiles. Since he was behind the camera, he could see what was being broadcast and she was made for primetime. The camera loved her.

With the interview completed, her face glowed as she walked toward him. "Whew. One down, ten to go. Did I sound like a rube?"

He flung his arm around her shoulders. "You did great. So calm and poised. People are going to be begging for last minute tickets."

"Oh!" She looked up at him. "There aren't any tickets left. We've been sold out for months."

"Well, that's good news. Next stop, *Big D* magazine. Let's go dazzle them with your brilliance."

"Or baffle 'em with my bullshit," she said, completing the infamous phrase.

Laughing, he opened the door for her.

At the magazine's offices, he sat in a corner and drank a cup of coffee as Risa answered questions about breast cancer and the gala set for the weekend. At both interviews, she'd been coy when answering questions about the mysterious Breast Cancer Diamond. She swore she hadn't even seen it yet, and that the jewelry designer would only provide the drawing. The unveiling would occur Saturday night at the gala fundraiser.

He knew Risa well. She'd gotten better at her lying, but he was sure only he realized it. She was good, but his BS detector was strong. She not only knew the exact carat count of that diamond, but the exact cut and style of the necklace.

He didn't know a whole lot more than the general public about the stone. Discovered a couple of years ago at the famous Argyle Diamond Mine in northwest Australia, after final cutting, the stone weighed fourteen carats. The value of the stone could only be estimated since the sale had been made to a private collector and the terms of the deal had been held in confidence. An estimation of the stone valued it at between eight-hundred-thousand and one million dollars *per carat*. That was some serious jack.

And the thing that ate at his craw was that *she* could afford to buy the damn stone for herself, but it was completely out of his reach, financially. She would always be able to give herself whatever she wanted.

Trevor was a modern man. One-hundred-percent in agreement with equal rights and equality of the sexes. He was actually proud of everything she'd accomplished, especially knowing that she and her sister could have chosen to follow the idle, carefree lifestyle of the very wealthy. Instead, she'd dedicated her life to service.

No, what bugged the crap out of him was the same stone bruise he'd had as a teen. He would always be financially limited in what he could provide her. There was nothing she couldn't get on her own.

Glancing to the back of the room where the interview was winding down, he watched as she laughed at something the reporter said. The shine of her eyes, the tilt of her lips, and sound of her laughter stirred areas inside him no other woman had ever touched, and he doubted ever would.

Chapter Five

W hen Trevor had first reviewed Risa's speaking schedule for Wednesday, he'd thought her quite smart to have built in a lunch engagement, killing two birds with one stone, so to speak. However, now as he sat at a table near the back of the meeting room for the local civics club, he changed his mind. Risa had been placed at a table with seven men, each one battling for a private word, or more, with her. And she did not disappoint. She moved salad around in her bowl as she spoke with the man to her left. Then, she shifted the entrée around on the plate while answering more questions than he would have had patience for. Through it all, she smiled and nodded and thoroughly charmed the men at her table to the point they seemed reluctant to allow her to leave her seat and begin her speech. However, at last, she rose and strode confidently to the podium.

He leaned back in his chair and watched her work her magic with the crowd. Her talk was basically the same one she'd given everywhere they'd stopped, except speaking to a live audience made her more alive, more animated. Her face glowed with excitement when she spoke about cancer trials and positive results. The sparkle in her eyes appeared as though a million fireflies were shining from inside. She gestured in concert with the words, making it appear she was directing a complicated sonata. She had the men and women, those community leaders, in the palm of her beautiful hand. He bet she could have sold a bunch of tickets to that Saturday event, had there been any available.

Once finished with the luncheon appointment and back in his SUV, she slumped against the door with a long sigh.

He shot her a quick glance as he signaled to make a turn. "You doing okay?"

She rolled her face toward him without lifting her head. "Sure. Just…I don't know…tired of using my words today."

"Adulting is so hard, right?"

She laughed. "Totally."

"How much of that lunch actually transferred from the plate into your mouth?"

One corner of her mouth quirked up. "Some."

"Some? Or very little?"

"You were watching me." The tension around her eyes relaxed. He never gave a woman's world much thought, but it made sense that knowing someone was watching out for her would be comforting.

"Of course, I was. That's what I was hired to do."

And while that statement was true, he also knew that his gaze would be on her any time they were in the same room. She drew him. After all these years, she still fascinated him. Unfortunately, the time apart hadn't really resolved the issue that had separated them.

Her gaze shifted back to the road. "True. We've got a couple of hours before we need to be at the radio station. Would you mind if we ran by my office so I can see what's been piled on my desk so far?"

He wrapped his hand around the back of her neck. "You're the boss." He gave her neck a gentle squeeze. "Wow. You're tense, babe."

"Tired. There's a difference.' She raised a hand to point. "Turn at the upcoming light and head to my office, okay?"

"No problem." He turned and followed her directions to a complex of medical buildings. After parking in the sport reserved for her, they took the elevators up to the second floor.

Making their way down to her office involved numerous pauses for accolades on the morning program and promises to listen to her live radio interview during the drive home.

She pointed toward a small kitchen break area. "You can wait in there."

He smiled. "Sweetheart, where you go, I go. Lead on."

Her shoulders slumped with a sigh. "But my office is a mess."

Picturing her immaculate home, he scoffed.

"What? A piece of paper out of place? Go on. I'm sure I can find somewhere to sit."

"Don't say I didn't warn you."

To say her office was a mess would be akin to noting that bombs had a tendency to move things around. On second glance, he wondered if some type of bomb had gone off. Files and papers covered the top of the desk, type of wood unknown because it couldn't be seen. Row after row of books filled the shelves, along with dozens of pictures of Risa with various dignitaries. Trevor had thought he'd become quite jaded, but damn! Once again, he was impressed, and maybe even a little intimidated by how much she'd accomplished and how much more he knew she'd do through her lifetime. Among all the celebrity photos were pictures of Risa with women, most without hair but wearing huge smiles.

"Those were patients," she said softly.

He turned toward her. "Were?"

"Yeah. Most of them." A weary sigh escaped. "I keep those around to remind myself why I do this, why I've sacrificed so much for my career." She leaned back in her chair. "See the one in the yellow blouse?"

He nodded.

"Rhonda Compton. Twenty-eight. No family history of any type of cancer. By the time her breast cancer was detected, it had metastasized to her liver and brain. She fought so hard but only lasted about six months. Left behind two young sons and a devastated husband." She rose and walked to stand beside him. "This patient was one of the lucky ones." She pointed to a thin woman in a bright blue blouse. "We caught her cancer so early that we killed it with chemo and a lumpectomy. She's about three years clear now and I don't expect to see her again, or at least not for the same cancer."

"How do you remember all them?" He put an arm around her, and she leaned into his side, letting him hold her.

"I don't remember them all. Some come in and are back home so fast, I can barely remember their names."

"The lucky ones," he ventured.

"Yeah. Then there are the ones like Rhonda." She picked up the picture of the first patient she'd talked about. "These make me so mad, I'm even more determined to fight. I'll find better ways to destroy these cancers before they take people who are just too young to die." She set the picture on the shelf. "I'm ready to go if you are. There's nothing here that can't wait until Monday." She stepped from his embrace and walked back to her desk. He lowered his arm to his side missing the feel of her touching him, of her scent filling his senses.

"I'm ready when you are. I'll check in with my office later."

The drive-time talk radio show went much like the earlier three events. When it was done, he realized how wan her face looked. At first, he blamed it on the harsh lighting but when the environmental lighting changed, her paleness remained.

"You need to eat," Trevor said. Taking her hand,

he led her toward the car. "You look like you're about to collapse."

"I'm just tired. After a good night's sleep, I'll be as good as new."

"I have a better idea. Dinner first and then I'm tucking you in bed."

She stopped and turned to look at him. "Exactly what are you proposing?"

Risa's heart lodged inside her throat. Was he finally putting his cards on the table and asking her to go to bed with him?

If so, what should she say?

He arched a brow. "Dinner and then we go back to your place, where I will make sure you're in bed so you'll get a good night's rest."

Disappointment settled thick in her belly. Even though she didn't want to admit it, she was exhausted, but she knew an evening in bed with Trevor would wake her up. Too bad he wasn't thinking along the same lines.

"What are you hungry for?" he asked.

You.

That's what she should have said. Instead, she replied, "I'm sure there's a casserole in the freezer at my place. We can nuke something there. Besides, I'm not really hungry."

Once they were inside her penthouse, Trevor had a few words with Sue, who waved and left.

Risa kicked off her shoes and dropped onto the sofa. "I don't think I can move."

Trevor took the chair closest to her. "You were very impressive today, Dr. McCool."

Turning her head toward him, she smiled. "Thank you. I have to be honest. I've enjoyed having you around today, but I'm embarrassed that I think I probably overreacted to this week."

"How so?"

"As you pointed out, my building is super secure. No one can steal anything, plus the Breast Cancer Diamond necklace isn't even here. I feel stupid making you stay here at night."

Trevor leaned forward, resting his forearms on his thighs. His gaze was steady. "Are you asking me to leave?"

Her stomach quivered at the deep, serious tone of his voice. "I'm not sure what I'm asking."

"I'm not leaving, Risa. I'm here to stay."

She wasn't sure exactly what he was saying. Was he here, as in her apartment? Or here, as in her life? She was too much of a wuss to ask.

They finally settled on a chicken casserole, salad and hot rolls for dinner. She moaned as she swallowed the last bite.

"Man, I didn't think I was hungry until I took that first bite. I need to remember to mark this casserole down for the future." She set her fork in her plate. "Why don't you go to the living room while I put these dishes away."

He stood and picked up his plate. "Give me yours. I wanted to go brew a fresh cup of coffee anyway."

After stacking her plate on top of his, he headed to the kitchen, Risa on his heels.

"Coffee? At this hour? Won't the caffeine keep you awake?"

"Nope." He put a coffee pod into the brewer and pushed start. "You want a cup?"

"Too late for me." She refilled her wine glass then leaned against the counter and watched him. When he bent over to stand the plates in the dishwasher, his pants pulled tight across his rear. Her gaze fastened on his firm butt, and her hands itched to touch it. She had the same reaction to his muscles flexing under his shirt. Her mouth watered at the vision. As a boy, he'd been cute, but as a man, he was devastatingly handsome.

"Okay, that's it." He collected his coffee and turned toward her. "You okay? You have an odd expression on your face."

She gulped down a splash of wine. "Oh yeah. I'm great."

They carried their drinks to the living room and took positions at each end of the sofa.

Risa propped her feet on the cushion beside her. "My shoes were little torture devices today."

"But they looked good, right?"

She grinned. "Right."

He scooted down until her feet were in his lap. "I bet I can help." Using his thumbs, he dug into the arch of her right foot, pressing and rubbing at the knots there.

She groaned. "Oh, damn. That feels so good."

"You relax, and let me see if I can help."

He massaged both feet, working the stiffness and soreness from muscles and tendons that weren't used to being shoved into high heeled shoes for hours. As each minute passed, Risa's body relaxed and melted more into the softness of her sofa. Her eyes fluttered shut as she soaked in the feel of his hands on her again after so many years.

Then, his fingers were on her ankles, moving in sensual circles around and around as he moved his hands higher on her legs. He worked on the tension in her calves, his thumbs diving deep into her flesh and the tightness there. Her legs grew limp and heavy under his relentless rubdown. She widened the space between her legs and he wasted no time moving his hands further up her legs to her knees, and then her thighs.

Her sex grew heavy. Moisture dampened her panties.

"Risa. I'm going to kiss you. Stop me now if you don't want me to."

When she opened her eyes, her gaze met his. His eyes were hooded and dark with lust. His lips were only millimeters from her mouth. She lifted her hand and threaded her fingers through his hair and pulled him toward her. As their lips met, her eyelids closed, the sensation of his taste overwhelming every sense.

His fingers stroked up and down her neck as he took the kiss deeper and wetter. A low groan vibrated in his chest.

She widened her legs again to allow his body

between her thighs, and then she wrapped her legs around him. Hard, rigid flesh pressed against her center. Her hips arched against him and then ground firmly against his cock.

He glided his mouth off her lips, leaving kiss after kiss along her cheeks, her jawbone, and then down her neck. She tossed back her head to give him more access to her neck, to anything he wanted. She skated her hands down his back to his ass—the firm, round ass she'd admired in the kitchen. Those hard glutes felt as good as they'd looked.

Through the shifting and arching of her hips, her skirt had worked its way up until it barely covered her panties. He shoved the linen material out of the way. His fingers danced along the damp silk of her underwear, rubbing and pushing the sodden crotch between the seam of her sex. Onc finger worked the satiny material into her opening. She moaned and hunched against his hand, so engaged in lust she could barely think.

"Trevor," she said against the flesh of his neck. "God, Trevor. I've missed you." She ran her tongue down the tendon in his neck to his shoulder. She bit and sucked at the salty tissue.

Arousal built inside. Her hips pumped, pushing against his hand, his fingers. She pressed her head against the pillow as she neared the top. Then he put his mouth on her sex, sucked her through the soaked silk of her panties before shoving the material inside her with his tongue.

And then she peaked. Waves of electric jolts

jumped from cell to cell as she climaxed. She called out his name, the name of the only man who'd ever made her feel like this.

As she floated back to earth, she released a contented sigh. "Wow." She looked up at Trevor, his face so beautiful, yet so serious. "Wow," she repeated.

He straightened her skirt over her thighs. "Tomorrow will be another long day. You should probably get some rest." He stood and held out a hand, which she took. He pulled her to her feet. "Good night." He released her hand and began walking away.

"Trevor." Her heart clogged her throat making it hard to speak. What had she done? Why was he leaving?

He stopped but didn't turn.

"Where are you going?"

"I have some calls to make, some work to do." He still didn't look at her.

"What…what did I do wrong?"

"Babe. You didn't do anything wrong. You could *never* do anything wrong." He looked over his shoulder, his gorgeous face sad. "That shouldn't have happened. I lost control, and it won't happen again. I'm sorry." He strode quickly away, never looking back.

She spent a long night of tossing and turning. In the morning, it took more than the dab of concealer she usually used to hide the dark circles. No aroma of fresh coffee met her as she made her way to the kitchen.

"Good morning," a chipper Sue greeted her. "Hope you got some good sleep."

Risa frowned. "Where's Trevor?"

"I'm your escort for today. Trevor had some business to take care of, and I got the lucky draw to spend the day with you. You look great, by the way. Super color on you."

Risa glanced down at the hot pink suit she'd put on and then back at Sue, still a little confused. "Thanks. Will Trevor join us today at some point?"

Sue shrugged. "No clue. He called me at about four this morning, gave me this assignment, and took off when I got here." She glanced around. "This is an awesome place. You are one lucky gal."

"I suppose." She went to the single serve coffee pot and put in a fresh pod. "You want some coffee?"

"Nope." Sue gestured with a large to-go cup. "Extra-large Diet Coke. My caffeine delivery of choice."

As unsettling as last night had been, finding Trevor gone and Sue in his place threw Risa's world even more off-kilter. She was sure Sue could handle anything that might arise, and hadn't she had the thought that maybe having someone with her all week was overkill?

"You know, Sue, I was just saying to Trevor last night that having a bodyguard seemed like an overreaction. I don't have much today, and there's no reason for you to tie up your day with me. I can do all my running around solo."

"Sorry, but when Trevor tells me to stay with you, I stay with you."

Risa drew in a deep breath. "I'll call him. Really. This is a total waste of your time."

"You can call, but I've known him a long time. Once bossman makes up his mind, it's impossible to change."

"Still…" Risa found Trevor's number in her cell and dialed.

"EyeSpy, International. This is Becky. How can I help you?"

"This is Risa McCool. I'm trying to reach Trevor, Trevor Mason."

"Good morning, Dr. McCool. I'm sorry, but Trevor isn't available. Is this an emergency?"

Risa looked at Sue, who arched one perfectly waxed brow.

"No, no emergency. I just won't need your services today. Tell Trevor that I'm sending Sue back to the office."

"I'll tell him."

Risa clicked off. "There. You're free to go."

Sue shrugged. "Trevor isn't going to be happy."

"Yeah, well, you don't always get what you want in life. Thanks for coming over. I'll walk you to the front door."

Sue retrieved a bag she'd left at the dining table. "Okay then. Call if you need anything."

"I'm sure I'll be fine."

Risa locked the door behind Sue, her emotions in

a whirl. She didn't need a stupid bodyguard. Not Trevor, not Sue. She didn't need anyone.

Her noon television interview came and went, and even if someone had put a gun to Risa's head, she couldn't have told them what the questions were or what she'd said. For all she remembered, she could have told the world her grandmother's recipe for moonshine.

She had lunch in her office while sorting through messages and mail. Her heart dropped when she recognized the handwriting on one envelope. Norman Compton, Rhonda's husband. He'd written her half-a-dozen times, each letter angrier than the last. Today's was no exception. His wife was dead. He'd lost his job due to continued absences, and now, Rhonda's parents were asking for custody of the children. Everything was Risa's fault for letting his wife die.

For some reason, Mr. Compton had gotten it into his mind that because they hadn't had insurance, Risa hadn't done all she could for his wife, or that if they'd had money, there were treatments Risa could have used that would have saved Rhonda. Of course, that was false. In fact, one of the reasons Risa had gotten behind the gala for Saturday was that much of the funding would go to help pay for cancer treatments for uninsured women.

In Rhonda Compton's case, no amount of money could have saved her life. The cancer had been widespread throughout her body. Risa had tried everything, but nothing had slowed the progression. Death had come swiftly, leaving a family in ruins.

She stashed the letter in her briefcase to put with the other letters she'd received. When the gala was behind her, she'd get some help for Mr. Compton. He wasn't a threat to her, but she feared he was a threat to himself.

Chapter Six

R isa's heart raced at the thought that she would
finally see the finished Breast Cancer Diamond
necklace. The plan was to place the finished necklace
on display at the Dallas Museum of Art, and remove it
annually for the Breast Cancer Diamond Gala. The
gala had been around for a number of years, under-
written by the McCool Foundation. However, the
addition of the Breast Cancer Diamond had shot
publicity and interest in the event through the roof
this year. At fifty-thousand dollars per ticket, the gala
always sold out, but this year, the tickets were gone in
record time. The planning committee had allocated an
additional one-hundred tickets and those had sold
within hours.

Risa parked outside Manfrey & Associates. Inside
awaited the finished necklace. She could hardly wait to
see what Greg Manfrey had done with the stone. At
this time, only Greg, her family and she knew that
Risa had bought the pink diamond and commissioned

the necklace. The uncut stone had been a bargain at only two million dollars. After the pink stone was cut and polished and set in eighteen-karat gold with accompanying pink and white diamonds, the estimated value of the necklace was closer to fifteen to twenty million dollars. She'd insured the necklace for the full twenty million. Although Risa told herself the necklace was an investment, she also knew she'd never sell.

Entrance to the jeweler's store was via a locked door. She rang the bell and waited. Momentarily, she was admitted to a foyer and waited for a second door to be unlocked. Once inside, the aroma of roses filled her nose.

"Risa," Greg said, coming from behind a curtain. "Who is the gentleman following you?"

Risa frowned. "I don't know what you're talking about. What man?"

Concern filled his expression. "The small man. Come. Take a look. He might still be out there."

Risa followed the older man to a back room where monitors sat lined up on a shelf.

"There. See?" Greg pointed to a still shot on a monitor. "He pulled up right behind you."

Risa squinted at the tiny screen. She didn't recognize the man. His body was short and stocky. His hair looked long and unkept. His clothes were dirty and wrinkled. Nothing about him was familiar.

"I have no idea who that is."

Manfrey jumped from camera to camera but the man was no longer there. "He's gone. He was probably headed to one of the other stores in the area. Sorry. Didn't mean to frighten you."

She smiled and touched the older man's arm. "You didn't. Probably nothing. Now, I'm dying to see the necklace."

His smile was quick. "Of course. I'll get it. Let's go back to the showroom where the lighting is better."

Risa took a final look at the monitors, focused in on the small, baby-blue Mini-Cooper and grinned. Did Sue really think she could hide in that tiny car of hers? Yes, she'd dismissed the woman, but knowing Trevor, he'd probably insisted Sue tail her all day anyway.

She went back to the lobby and took a seat. The idea that someone, other than Sue, was following her was ridiculous, right? The fact she was running around with bodyguards all week had been well publicized.

For just a second, she wished she had allowed Sue to ride around with her today. Making the poor woman play tag with her was silly, but before she spent much time on that thought, Greg came from the back with a large, blue velvet case.

"Here it is," he said and opened the top.

She gasped.

When she left twenty minutes later, the store's security guard escorted her to her car. Under her wiper, a small piece of paper flapped in the wind.

"Oh man, Dr. McCool. Looks like you have a ticket," the guard said. "Give it to me, and the store will take care of it."

Risa pulled the paper from the windshield and quickly determined it was a note, not a ticket. "It's fine. Someone left me a note. No biggie. Thanks for walking me out."

She slipped into her car and locked the door, still a little unnerved that Greg had thought she'd been followed by some guy. She glanced around. Her car was the only one sitting in the lot, and there were no other people in the area. Sue was probably parked out of sight and would try to slip in behind her in traffic.

The paper crinkled loudly in her tomb-quiet car as she straightened it to read the words scrawled in pencil.

RICH BITCHES GET WHAT THEY DESERVE

Anger flared through her. This wasn't the first time she'd been targeted because of her parents' money. One of the reasons she hadn't wanted to be the chairperson for the gala was that she knew she'd be front and center for the publicity. Obviously, someone had recognized her from all the television appearances or the advertising for the gala and thought they'd let her know just what they thought of her. There were some mean people in the world.

She wadded up the note and tossed it behind her seat with the rest of her trash. That's where it belonged. She started her car and pointed it toward home.

Her condo felt empty when she arrived, which matched how hollow she felt inside. Trevor had only been there for a couple of days, and yet, she missed him. She wandered down to the bedroom where he'd stayed. The bed was made. The counter in the bathroom was clear. Clean, dry towels hung from the racks. If she hadn't known differently, she'd have thought no one had occupied the room ever. But when she shut her eyes and drew in a breath, she could swear she could still smell him. Not a cologne scent. Not a soap scent. An aroma that was pure Trevor. Drawing in a deep breath, she walked out and shut the door.

She ate a salad for dinner and sat on the terrace for a couple of hours watching the lights of Dallas as they blinked on for the evening. What her parents had paid for the penthouse suites was obscene, but she loved the night view and the layers of security the building provided. She thought about the note from that afternoon and got angry again. Whoever had left that note didn't know her, didn't know how hard she worked, how much of herself she gave to her work. The person saw her going into an exclusive jeweler and made assumptions about her and her life. They looked at her and believed money solved everything, but it didn't. Children still got sick. Patients still died. Love went unreturned. What they didn't understand was that, sometimes, money itself could be the barrier between people, like it had been for Trevor and her.

A tear rolled down her cheek. Her chest hurt. Her stomach ached. Her heart… Well, it was simply shattered. Shit. She swiped at the dampness on her face. Damn him. Why couldn't he accept her as she was? Mousy brown hair, green eyes, and a trust fund the size of a treasury for a small country.

The house phone in the kitchen rang. She hurried to it, hoping against hope it might be Trevor.

"Hello?"

"Dr. McCool. This is Jasper from downstairs. You have guest asking to come up. Sue Lee."

Her shoulders sagged from the weight of her disappointment. She checked the time. Almost ten. She'd been sitting on the terrace for hours. "Send her up."

She went to the front door and waited for Sue.

"Hi, Dr. McCool," Sue said brightly. "Did you have a good day?"

"Hi, Sue. I'm surprised to see you."

"Trevor sent me to check on you. He wanted to make sure everything's okay."

Risa leaned against the doorframe. "Everything is fine. Are you staying or just dropping by to report back?"

Sue smiled. "Trevor would like me to stay for a while."

"Come on in." Risa stepped back and allowed the bodyguard to enter. "Make yourself at home. I think I'm going to read in my bedroom."

"Sure thing. Have a good night."

Risa left Sue in the living room and headed for her bedroom. She didn't need a perky, petite woman tonight. She needed a muscular, brooding Trevor. Since that didn't seem to be an option, she took a shower and climbed between her sheets. Two pages into the latest cancer journal, her eyes slammed shut, and she drifted off.

Her eyes opened at the touch. Her room was pitch dark. She was on her stomach, her hands stretched over her head. His scent wrapped around her. He was here.

A large hand with thick fingers slid up the inside of her thigh. She spread her legs giving him access to her center. A heavy body lowered onto her. Lips pressed against her neck. The tip of a tongue circled the outer rim of her ear.

"Damn you, Risa," Trevor's deep voice rasped into her ear. "Damn you for sucking me back in. I can't stay away."

Her heart tripped. He felt as ensnared as she did. "I don't want you to stay away. I want you here with me, over me, in me."

His weight shifted as he moved to her side. His fingers stroked her inner thigh as he moved his hand toward her slit. He groaned when he discovered she wore nothing. He dipped his fingers into her creamy arousal and then inserted one finger into her steamy sex.

She moaned and arched her hips off the bed.

His finger was joined by a second thrusting deep inside her canal. She pushed against his fingers, needing more.

He shifted on the bed. The tip of his tongue touched the nape of her neck and then he slowly ran it down each vertebra. She pulled her knees under her, raising her ass into the air, giving him access to every inch of her body. He owned it, even if he didn't realize that yet. She was his. Always was and always would be.

His mouth replaced his fingers, licking and biting her flesh, then sucking away the sting. He flicked his tongue inside her, driving it as deep as he could. She moaned, unable to stop her hips from pumping back and forth. Then his lips found her clit and latched on, sucking and drawing it between his teeth. When he bit softly, she screamed as her climax hit. She rode it up and over, falling and shaking with the force.

When her quivering slowed, she heard the tear of a foil pouch then felt the large head of his cock pressing at her entrance. Still on her knees, she arched her back as he stretched her to take him deep. Once he was fully seated, he pulled back and thrust firmly, his balls slapping her flesh with each stroke.

His mouth was next to her ear as he groaned with each plunge. "Risa," he whispered. "Risa. My God, Risa. You feel so good even though I know this is wrong for both of us."

He drove roughly inside her, driving her breath from her lungs. His tongue ran around her ear. His heavy breaths sent chills down her spine.

"No matter what happens," he said as he pumped into her. "Know that there will never be another woman like you. Never."

He thrust a couple of times while applying finger pressure to her clit. Her second orgasm came faster and harder than the first. Tears filled her eyes and rolled down her cheeks.

With the next thrust, he held tight inside her as he came with a force that rocked her and her bed.

When he was done, he slipped from the bed and did not return.

Friday morning, Sue met her with an annoyingly bright smile. "Good morning, Dr. McCool."

Risa frowned. "Did you stay here last night?"

Sue nodded. "Yes. Trevor ordered me to stay, and I did, but it was quiet. I hope you don't mind that I used the guest room. Trevor said it would be fine."

Risa looked around the kitchen. "Is Trevor here?"

"No, ma'am. He checked in last night after you went to bed. Said he wanted to check all the locks and security, but then he left."

"Oh." If it weren't for the ache in muscles that hadn't been used in years, she would have thought last night had been a dream. Trevor had been there, with her, in her.

"So, what are we doing today?" Sue asked, her chipper voice making Risa wince.

"Picking up my dress, meeting with gala security one more time and getting highlights in my hair."

"And the necklace? Do we need to pick that up today?"

Risa pulled her coffee mug from the single serve machine, ignoring the question about the necklace. "You riding around with me? Or following me in your car like you did yesterday?"

Sue's cheeks reddened. "You saw me? Damn it."

"I saw your cute Mini-Cooper parked on the

street, but I liked knowing you were there. I felt very secure with you mirroring my every move."

"Maybe you might keep it to yourself that you saw me...?" Sue said, wrinkling her nose. "The guys at the office would never let me live it down."

Risa pretended to close a button on her lips.

"Thank you," Sue said. "I owe you."

Risa thought about Sue letting Trevor in last night, the incredible sex and then said, "No, I think we're square."

Risa rode with Sue, letting Sue do all the driving while Risa rested up from the previous night. After picking up Risa's dress for the event, they headed over to the Grand Millennium Hotel of Dallas, the host hotel for the gala, where the final security meeting would be held. When Risa entered the hotel's board-room, the meeting was just beginning with Trevor taking the lead. Dressed in black slacks, a black T-shirt that stretched tight across his broad shoulders and an EyeSpy windbreaker, the sight of him made her mouth watered. Her hands clenched at her side. Her heart flipped at the sound of his voice. Her gaze ate him up. How could a feeling this strong be wrong? And even more, why did he think it wrong? That made no sense.

She took a seat at the table and listened as each person went through the security details for the evening. Between the uniformed security and the undercover security, she felt comfortable that the gala guests would be safe, not to mention the Breast Cancer Diamond.

"Don't you agree?"

The question jolted Risa back to reality. "Um, I missed the question. What did you ask?"

Trevor's gaze met hers. Heat roared inside her. Lust leapt from cell to cell until she was consumed. Blood rushed below her waist and fluid dampened her panties.

"I was explaining that I'd be attending as your escort, and that would add an extra layer of protection for the diamond."

"Oh, yes. Right." She pulled her gaze off Trevor to look around the room at the others involved in making sure the event was secure. "I'm impressed with all the layers of security you've put in place. I appreciate all your hard work." She stood, and every man in the room stood with her. "I have another appointment so I'll leave this in your hands. I'll see you all tomorrow night."

TREVOR'S GUT SQUEEZED AS HE WATCHED RISA EXIT the room. All the men in the room turned to observe her as well. Jealousy flared because he knew every man in the room wanted her, would kill to have Risa McCool the way he had last night. Naked. Vulnerable. Taking his cock inside her. Driving her to orgasm over and over, and it still wasn't enough. He had hoped that having her again would ease the overwhelming need thrumming through him, but it hadn't. If anything, she was the drug he couldn't give up.

The meeting ended and he raced his truck

through the streets of Dallas to his office. He needed a drink, a stiff shot of bourbon, but until this gala was over, only black coffee was on his menu. Slamming his office door, he paced the room in agitation. He'd come back to Texas for family. He'd thought that maybe his issues with Risa were in the past, and they could reconnect as friends. Now? He didn't think that was possible.

He'd grown up in a lower middle-class family. Money had been tight. His parents had lived paycheck to paycheck. No way could he have gone to college without that football scholarship, but even that hadn't paid for everything. He'd watched his folks struggle to make it work for him, taking extra jobs, working over-time when possible, squeezing every penny so he would have spending money, but after a year, he couldn't let them kill themselves for him. He had a younger brother who needed his parents, too. So, he'd dropped out and signed up.

Risa had never understood his dropping out of college, never understood how it had killed him when she'd offered to pay for dinners out, or dates. Other guys might have taken Risa's money and the football scholarship and continued on, but not Trevor. If he couldn't pay for something, he did without. She'd never made an issue of money, her having it and him not. But she'd deserved so much more than he could have provided. He'd thought if he left, she'd be free to find someone who could give her the world.

Instead, she'd thrown herself into her studies. Sure, she'd dumped him via a letter, but hadn't he made the first move by leaving her? And now, fifteen years later, she was still the only woman whose name was tattooed on his heart, and he still wasn't good enough for her.

So what was he going to do about it?

Chapter Seven

Trevor went home, tried to get his mind off Risa, off his craving for her body, her touch. Television couldn't hold his attention. Neither could the latest spy novel. Nothing took his mind off Risa. Her scent. Her taste. Her touch. He was driving himself crazy with need. Finally at midnight, he drove to her condo. From the parking lot, he telephoned Sue.

"On the way up," he said. "I'm taking this shift. You go home and get some rest for tomorrow night."

"Whatever you say," Sue replied.

The night guard knew him and let him take the public elevator up to the penthouse.

Sue opened the door with, "All yours, boss," and left.

Trevor locked the door and walked around the condo. Locked up tight. Sue had been a good hire. Someone he trusted, and that said a lot. Outside of his SEAL team, there weren't many people he trusted with his life.

He toed off his shoes at the door to Risa's bedroom and soundlessly opened the door. She lay on her side. The full moon kissed her beautiful face. Her auburn hair spread across her pillow and shone in the nightlight. God, she was stunning. His heart ached just looking at her. His hands balled into fists then relaxed against his leg. His breathing synced with the rise and fall of her chest. He turned and made his way back to the glass room overlooking the downtown lights of Dallas. They sparkled like polished gemstones.

What was he doing here? It was torture being so close and denying himself her touch.

Arms wrapped around his waist. Risa's hands stroked his abdomen. "You came back."

Her voice was raspy with sleep and sexy as hell.

"I tried to stay away, but I couldn't."

"Good. I want you here. Don't you get that?"

He set his hands on top of hers. "Why me, Risa?"

"It's always been you. Didn't you know?" She stepped around him, letting her arms glide around his waist. She stood naked in front of him. Her erect nipples brushed his shirt.

His hands slid from her waist to her rear, his fingers digging into the flesh there.

"From the moment I saw you, I knew it was you." She laid her hand on her chest. "In here. I knew. And in all the years we've been apart, that never changed. Even when you left me for the Navy, you were still here."

"Then why did you send me a letter breaking it off?"

"I was young and stupid. I thought if I wrote you off, told you to go away, my heart would fall in line. I would date other men, find someone to fill the hole you left." She shook her head. "Never happened. You hold the key to me. No one else."

Rising on her toes, she kissed him. A jolt of lust shot through his veins. Blood rushed to his cock. Just a simple kiss had him wanting to beg. She broke the kiss and looked down at her hands at the waistband of his slacks. She pushed the button through the opening and eased the zipper over his hard dick. Releasing the material, she let his slacks slide down and pool around his ankles. She wedged her fingertips under the elastic of his boxers and, as she lowered herself to her knees, took them with her. He lifted one foot and then the other, allowing her to sweep the material to the side.

His cock stretched upward and bounced on his abdomen. When she licked her lips, he groaned. She wrapped her fingers around the base of his dick and flicked out her tongue to lick the head. He locked his knees to remain standing. Slowly, she lowered her mouth over his hard flesh. He watched his cock disappear into her mouth, and he had to brace himself with a hand on the window. Standing in a moonlit room, the most incredible woman on her knees in front of him, taking him as deep as she could, felt like a dream. If it was, it was a dream from which he never wanted to awaken.

Threading his fingers into her soft waves, he held her head as his hips pistoned in and out. "Damn, baby," he said with a long groan. "That feels so good."

Tightening her hands around his dick, she moved up and down in concert with her mouth, sucking on him so hard he wanted to let his eyes roll back in his head. She released his cock and used her tongue to lick around the head, then her teeth to nibble along the rim, before flattening her tongue on the side and licking him from base to head.

His knees gave a little under the relentless assault of her luscious mouth. His fingers tightened in her hair as he pulled the strands.

Her gaze rolled up and met his. "Come," she said. "Let me have all of you in my mouth." She wrapped her lips around the head and sank down on his cock.

"Babe," he groaned. His hips thrust into her warm embrace. His cock found the back of her throat. He pulled out and pumped again, the orgasmic tension rising with each stroke, each suck, every lick. He held her head in both hands as he moved in and out rapidly, his climax hitting like a tornado. She took everything he had, swallowing everything he gave.

When his climax stilled, he reached down and pulled Risa to her feet, and then lifted her into his arms. He carried her to her bedroom and lay her on her bed.

"You are the love of my life," he said.

She held out her arms to him. After stripping off his shirt, he joined her in her bed.

"And you are mine," she said as they began to make love again.

RISA SHIELDED HER EYES FROM THE SUN THAT INSISTED on pouring through her window. Rolling over, she reached for Trevor only to find the bed empty. A peek from under her eyelids confirmed that she was alone. Flopping to her back, she stretched her arms over her head and laughed. Last night defied every fantasy she'd had.

After a quick shower, she wrapped herself in a robe and headed for coffee, only to be stopped by the sounds of laughter from her kitchen.

"And then what happened?" Wendy asked.

"Well, what do you think? We hauled ass out of there," Trevor replied, which made Wendy laugh again.

"Good morning," Risa said. "Wendy, what are you doing here so early?"

"Early? It's almost ten."

Risa paused. "You're kidding?" She whipped her gaze to the clock on the stove and read ten-fifteen. "Wow. I don't know when I've slept so late."

Wendy gave a little shrug. "Busy week or busy night?" she asked with a nudge on Trevor's shoulder.

His reply was a grin. "Morning. I've already had breakfast. You hungry?"

Risa shook her head and filled a coffee mug. "No. Maybe later." She took a long gulp of caffeine. "You still riding with us tonight, Wendy?"

"Yep. Everett will be at my place about six-thirty, and then we'll head over here. I was thinking drinks before we go…?"

Risa nodded. "That's fine."

Wendy stood. "I need to run. I want to get a work-out in this morning." She took two steps and turned back. "I can't believe I forgot. The necklace. How did it turn out?"

"Incredible. Want to see?"

"Hell, yeah."

"Wait," Trevor said, his eyebrows lowering. "That damn necklace is here? As in this condo?"

Risa smiled. "I brought it home yesterday."

"And you didn't think I needed to know that?"

She shrugged. "I wasn't worried. Until now, I was the only one who knew." Looking at her sister, she said, "Wait. I'll be right back."

When she headed for her bedroom, Trevor was on her heels.

"I can't believe you didn't mention you brought the necklace home. I need to get a couple of extra guys downstairs."

"Relax," she said. "It's fine. I didn't tell you because…" She pressed herself against his hard body and walked her fingers up his chest until her arms were around his neck. "I had much better things on my mind than talking about this necklace." Pressing her lips to his, she ran her tongue along the inside of his lower lip. "I can show Wendy the necklace later. What do you think?"

He caught her ass in both hands and lifted her until her legs were around his waist.

"Wendy," he shouted. "Let yourself out and lock the door."

"Fine, but you owe me."

They heard the door slam.

Risa licked up the side of his neck. "Yum." She leaned back far enough to open her robe. She was bare underneath. "I'd rather be wearing you."

He growled and kicked the bedroom door shut behind them.

Two hours later, the house phone rang announcing that Risa's nail tech was there to touch up her polish.

The afternoon passed in a blur. After the nail tech, the make-up artist came to do Risa's then Wendy's faces for the evening. Risa, who wasn't accustomed to wearing much more than powder and eyeliner, stared at herself in the mirror. The woman staring back looked like Risa, but oh, so much better.

At five, Risa's hair stylist came. When he was done, Risa's long hair had been swept up into curls and swirls that made her gasp with delight. Her hair dresser then used an entire can of hair spray to hold all the strands exactly where he wanted them. She figured it would take at least five shampoos to get all the gel and starch out, but she didn't care. For tonight, she looked like a princess.

Trevor left when the nail tech arrived, saying something about too much estrogen and fear of another manicure. He left two burly guards in the hall between her condo and Wendy's.

It was after six when Risa slipped her dress over her spandex support. The dress was light grey silk with pink roses embroidered from above her knees down to the hem. The pink thread was an identical match to the pink of the Breast Cancer Diamond. She was struggling to zip the back when there was a knock on her bedroom door.

"Yes?"

"It's me," Trevor said. "Can I come in?"

"Please. I need you to zip my dress."

He walked in and stopped dead in his tracks.

"What's wrong?" she looked up at him and smiled. "Wow," she said as she studied the most handsome man in the world in his midnight black tux. "You are gorgeous."

"I'm pretty sure I'll fade into the woodwork next to you," he said. "You are stunning."

"Yeah, well, don't get used to it. It took hours and lots of professional help to make me look like this."

He stepped toward her. "It's not the hair, or the makeup, or even the dress that makes you stunning, sweetheart. You just are."

Her heart swelled, making it hard to breathe. "Thank you."

"Now, where's this zipper?"

She turned her back, and he lowered the zipper to the top of her ass. His large, hot hands pressed into her back, his thumbs stroking up and down her spine. She swallowed against the lust rising in her throat.

"Up, not down," she choked out.

"In a minute." He pressed his mouth to her shoulder then moved to kiss the other side. She shivered under his touch. His lips caressed her back as he kissed his way down her spine to where his fingers rested on the top of her ass. The soft scrape of his beard had goose bumps popping up everywhere his mouth glided over her skin. As he pulled the slider up to close the zipper, his mouth kissed each inch before the dress closed over it.

The dress had an elaborate collar that stood up behind the back of her head. The neckline came over her shoulders and dipped low in the front, exposing her cleavage. Once the back was closed, Trevor turned her in his arms, and then stepped back. His gaze slid from her face, down to the dress's hem and back up. "Sadly, no one will even notice that multi-million dollar necklace tonight. You'll outshine it."

She smiled. "Bullshit, but thank you. Hold on. I'll grab the necklace."

Opening her underwear drawer, she lifted out the blue velvet box and flipped open the lid.

"Isn't it something?" she said, holding the large, pink diamond in the palm of her hand.

The pear-shaped, fourteen-carat pink diamond was fitted in eighteen-karat gold and dangled from a strand of ninety white and pink diamonds in leaf formations. The necklace looped around the neck and fastened in the front instead of at the back. The clasp was hidden among the diamond leaves.

As she placed the necklace on, Risa noticed a frown on Trevor's face. "You don't like it?"

He nodded. "It's incredible."

"Then why the frown?"

"It's nothing. I didn't even realize I was frowning." His lips arched into a smile, but she knew him well enough to see the smile never reached his eyes. "You are breathtaking. I'll be guarding you from the other men more than safeguarding the necklace."

Smiling, she ran her hand over his cheek. "I'm so glad you didn't shave this off. It makes me crazy when you kiss me." When he leaned in to kiss her, she held him off with a hand against his chest. "It took over an hour to make my face look like this."

"Sorry."

He was moving away when she caught his face between her hands and pulled him close.

"I get to do the kissing now. You can take over later." She lightly pressed her mouth to his.

He grinned. "I'll look forward to messing up your makeup, your hair and stripping that dress from you. Might be fun to see you in only a pink diamond."

"That can be arranged," she said with a chuckle and pulled him from her bedroom. "I put some champagne on ice for Wendy and Everett. They should be here any minute. Can you bring the bottle and four glasses to the sun room?"

"Sure," he was saying as the doorbell chimed.

"I'll go. You get the champagne?"

The front door opened before she got to it, and Wendy and Everett entered. She'd always wondered what her sister saw in Everett. He was vain, conceited, and had more clothes than she did, but tonight, all that paid off. Dressed in a black tux, his blond hair wearing more hairspray than hers, he looked like the rich financier he was. Wendy's red dress floated around her feet like fog. Her blonde hair had also been put into an uptwist, and their grandmother's tiara shone prominently from her crown. The strapless gown left her shoulders bare.

"Wow. You two clean up pretty good," Risa joked.

"I know," Wendy said with a laugh, and then she gasped. "Oh my, Risa. That necklace is mind-blowing."

Risa ran her fingers over the stone. "I know. Manfrey did more with the design than I ever could've imagined."

Trevor stepped up beside her. "Drinks on the sun porch."

As they walked back to the glass room, Risa's heart raced, and her stomach rolled over as she remembered being on her knees here last night. Trevor's large hand was on her waist and squeezed, making her aware he was thinking of the same thing.

"What's wrong?" Wendy asked. "You're all flushed."

"Nerves," Risa lied. "I hope tonight goes off without a hitch."

Trevor poured the champagne into four flutes and passed them out. "I'm sure it'll go great." He lifted his glass. "This is to us, Everett. We were smart enough to lock down these two beautiful women as our dates tonight."

"Here, here," Everett said with a chuckle and clinked Trevor's glass.

"To cancer research," Risa said. "May tonight haul in a ton of money for research and treatment."

"Amen," Wendy said, and they all clinked glasses and took a drink.

"Sit, sit," Risa said as she lowered herself to one of the sofas. "Did you get a chance to look over the silent auction items?"

"We were just talking about that as we were walking over," Everett said. "Impressive array."

"Thanks. I've twisted so many arms this past year, I'll owe favors for the rest of my life."

"Or until you start twisting arms again for next year," Wendy said.

Risa tilted her head. "Maybe. We'll see."

"What's your favorite item?" Trevor asked.

"Cowboys tickets, and not just the tickets but a sky box on the forty-yard line."

Trevor groaned. "Oh, brother. My dad would love those."

"Maybe you should bid on them," Risa suggested.

"Too rich for my blood, I'm afraid," Trevor said.

"You never know," Risa said.

The conversation moved into the Cowboys' record, and Risa sat back and watched Trevor. Those tickets would go for a few hundred thousand. She'd make a point of getting by and leaving what would have to be the winning bid.

The two couples left the condo at seven in a black stretch limousine. Trevor had arranged for the limo to be sandwiched between two of his company SUVs, and Risa felt quite secure. Due to the publicity, there were hundreds of people lined up outside the hotel to see the gala attendees as they exited cars and made their way up the stairs. As their limo pulled to a stop, Risa pressed her hand against her stomach.

"You okay?" Trevor asked.

"Nerves, I'm sure. My stomach is on a roller coaster ride."

"This evening will be a success beyond your wildest dreams. I promise."

Chapter Eight

Risa had prepared herself for the questions from reporters. What she hadn't prepared for was being blinded by the camera flashes. She pasted on a smile and hoped it looked more natural than it felt.

"This way, Risa," voices yelled as she turned to show off the incredible stone.

Someone broke through the crowd barrier and rushed toward her. Trevor grabbed her by her waist and lifted her off her feet. She found herself carried toward the hotel's entrance. A commotion behind her made her turn back as soon as her feet touched the ground again. Cops had a man on the ground, his arms twisted behind his back.

"What happened?" she asked.

Behind her, the guy was calling her name, declaring his love for her.

"You have a fan," Trevor said dryly, releasing her waist. "You know him?"

Risa stared and shook her head. "I've never seen him before."

Wendy linked her arm with Risa's. "Too many television appearances?"

"All I know is that next year, you get to be the spokesperson," Risa said. "You know I hate this stuff."

"No problem," Wendy said. "I'd love it."

"Let's head in. Dallas police have this under control," Trevor said.

Walking up the stairs leading to the hotel's entrance felt like walking back in time. Built during the Texas oil boom in the early 1900s, the Grand Millennium Hotel of Dallas had been abandoned and left to ruin until two years ago. The Wise family of Dallas had purchased the grand lady and spent millions renovating the hotel, giving it a modern interior while maintaining the hotel's history and charm. Uniformed bellmen opened the doors, and the two couples swept inside the high-domed lobby. Music from unseen speakers played softly in the background. Patrons and guests filled tables or stood at the lobby bar. Tonight's event was on the top floor ballroom, which was actually the top two levels of the hotel.

The elevator doors opened, and the two couples stepped inside. Trevor took Risa's hand and gave it a gentle squeeze. "Everything will be perfect. You'll see."

She exhaled the breath she'd been holding. "I hope so."

The lower ballroom was packed as they entered. Dinner and dancing would be on this level while the items for the silent auction had been staged on the second level. As Trevor and Risa made their way through the crowd, she was stopped frequently for small talk or hugs from friends. She noticed Trevor's gaze scanning the room, connecting on occasion with other men dressed in tuxedos and blending in with the crowd.

He never let her out of his sight and rarely removed his hand from the small of her back. She loved the feel of his broad hand as it warmed her flesh. Even more, the heat reminded her of the hot sex she'd had with him.

It took almost an hour to get upstairs to the silent auction. When Trevor stopped to speak with a guy she knew worked with EyeSpy, she took advantage of the separation to find the Dallas Cowboys tickets and skybox. She wrote in her bid, an amount in the six figures that would be hard for most people to top. She was determined to do this for Trevor and his dad. Hadn't he said how much his dad would love this?

"What are you doing?" he whispered in her ear.

She startled. "Nothing."

He looked at the bid, and his mouth dropped. "Risa. What are you thinking?"

"I'm thinking this would make a great Christmas present for you and your dad."

His jaw tightened. "You know how I feel about you spending money on me."

She put her hand on her hip. "And you know I love doing it."

"And once again, we find ourselves at the same

crossroads, having the same discussion. I live within my means, not yours."

"You're being ridiculous." She wanted to stomp her foot. "Grow up."

"Grow up?" He snorted. "Lady, you have some nerve."

The gong rang to indicate dinner was served. Risa whipped around and walked off. He was so stubborn.

She could barely swallow around the lump in her throat. She smiled, she chatted, but inside, fury burned. It was the past all over again. Her stomach bubbled with acid. Her hands shook with a combination of nerves and anger.

As coffee was being poured, her stomach threatened to make itself known. "I need to use the restroom," she whispered in Trevor's ear.

He nodded and stood, holding out his hand for hers. She placed her hand in his fingers and stood, just as a vicious cramp wracked her gut.

"Oh," she gasped.

His hand tightened. "Do you need to leave?"

"Just get me to a bathroom. I'm sure this will pass."

As they made their way across the room, she nodded and smiled at everyone but never slowed her determined march. He spoke into the mic attached to his sleeve, asking Sue to go into the ladies' room and clear it.

"Sue's making sure the room is safe for you."

"I don't care if it's empty. I have to go in there... now," she hissed into his ear. "And I mean, now."

Sue was exiting the hallway where the men's and ladies' rooms were located. With a nod, she stepped aside for Risa to hurry past.

"Please keep everyone out," Risa said to Sue. "And I mean everyone. God, this is embarrassing."

Sue stopped Trevor as he started down the hall. "She's fine. No one's in there. Give her some space," she heard Sue say.

Seven minutes later, Risa stood at the sink washing her hands when the door to the ladies' room slammed open and Trevor charged through.

"What?" she said with a frown.

"You alone?"

She looked at him and then at the empty restroom. "Um, yeah. What's going on?"

"Is Wendy in here with you?"

"No. Why would she be in here with me? And wouldn't you have seen her come down the hall?"

He lifted his sleeve to his mouth. "Negative on the ladies' room."

Risa's heart began to speed, and again, her stomach tightened. "Trevor, what the hell is going on?"

"Everett said that Wendy got a note from you saying you were sick and asking her to meet you. When she didn't return, he went looking for her."

"Meet me where? I didn't send her a note."

"Everett wasn't sure, but he thought downstairs in the lobby."

"So why are you in here?" Risa started for the door.

Trevor grabbed her arm. "You need to stay here where we can keep an eye on you."

"We? You mean EyeSpy? Forget it. If Wendy's in trouble, I need to be there."

"It could be a ploy to steal your necklace."

Risa absentmindedly fingered the large stone. "And maybe it's someone playing a game, and if it's not, and this is about the necklace, you don't think I'd toss this hunk of rock for my sister?"

She pulled her arm free and headed for the door. She'd just stepped into the small hallway that contained the men's and ladies' restrooms when she heard her name called.

"Dr. McCool."

She whirled around. A young man dressed in a waiter's uniform stood in the doorway to the hall.

"Some guy paid me a hundred bucks to give you this." He held out an envelope.

She rushed toward him, but Trevor got there first and snatched the paper from the guy's hand before she could.

"Give me that. It's for me, not you." She fumbled for the note, but he held it out of her reach.

Trevor's features hardened. "Angel, there is nothing I wouldn't do for you, but not this time. Let me read it."

When he tried to open the flap, she jerked the envelope out of his hands. "Just stop it, Trevor. If my sister is in trouble, I need to know."

She pulled the paper out and shared it with Trevor.

I HAVE YOUR SISTER. MEET US IN THE BOARDROOM ON THE SECOND FLOOR. COME ALONE.

Releasing her hold on the paper, Risa raced for the elevator, Trevor on her heels, calling orders into the mic in his sleeve.

She stabbed the elevator button but none of the cars were up on the twentieth floor where she was. She couldn't wait. The hotel was packed tonight, and waiting for an elevator car to arrive would take time she didn't have. Instead, she hurried to the exit, kicked off her shoes and started down the stairs.

"Goddamn it, Risa," Trevor muttered as he raced behind her toward the exit. "Have a little faith. I have men on every floor." Which was the last thing he wanted to yell in the stairwell and alert everyone there was a problem. As if the event's chairperson running through the ballroom wasn't enough of a sight, her flinging her shoes off and charging for the stairs was enough to have heads turning and questions asked.

"Risa," he yelled as he took the stairs two at a time. "Wait a minute."

"Can't."

He flung himself over the railing to the next set of steps and overtook his stubborn date. He grabbed her arm. "Slow down."

"Someone has my sister. I will not slow down." She jerked her arm but couldn't break his hold.

"One of my guys is holding the elevator on level eighteen for us."

"Why didn't you say so?" She spun toward the door marked eighteen and flew through it.

He shook his head and followed. She was going to be the death of him.

In the elevator on the way down, he took her hand and forced her to look at him. "Listen, Risa. This is my job. I'm good at my job. Let me do what I do best."

"It's my sister." Tears filled her eyes.

"I know." He pulled her head against his chest. "She'll be fine. Just let me work, okay?" When she didn't say anything, he put his fingers under her chin and lifted her face until their gazes met. "Trust me."

She nodded.

The doors opened, and they stepped out. Quickly, he glanced around. There was no action or movement. Music floated from the lobby bar. There was no one in the hall except a man wearing a doorman's uniform. Trevor gave the man a nod. A former SEAL from a different team but a man Trevor trusted. "Grant."

"Trevor."

"Anything?"

"Quiet as a church mouse, but I didn't open the boardroom door."

"Okay. Keep everyone else off the floor."

"Got it."

"You wait here," Trevor said to Risa.

"Yeah, that ain't gonna happen." She grabbed Trevor's arm. "If this is about the stupid necklace, give it to him and let him leave." Releasing his arm, she took a couple of steps down the hall toward the room where they'd held the security briefings.

"Damn it." Two long strides, and he was beside her.

"Wendy," she called through the door. "You in there?"

"I'm here," came the strained reply.

"Are you okay?" Risa asked.

"Yeah. He says you'd better be alone."

"I am." She shoved Trevor back just as the head of hotel security joined them.

"You know who's in there with her?" the hotel security guy asked Trevor.

"No clue, but I need to get in there before someone gets hurt."

"Risa?" Wendy called.

"Yeah?"

"We're coming out. He says if he sees anyone but you, he'll shoot me."

Risa gasped, and her hand went to her mouth. She whirled on Trevor. "Go away," she whispered. "I'll never forgive you if you make the guy shoot Wendy."

"He's not going to shoot her," Trevor said. "He wants you, not her. If he shoots her, he's gained nothing."

He pulled a rounded piece of plastic from his pocket. "Here. Put this in your ear," he said to Risa. "I'll be close enough to hear what's going on, and I'll be able to talk to you." He turned her toward him. "You're determined to do this, aren't you?"

She pushed the earpiece in her ear and nodded.

He kissed her and stepped around the corner out of sight. "Okay, teams, listen up. Alpha team, go to the lobby and wait. Take no action. Beta team, take the third floor and be ready to move. Delta team, cover the elevators. No one goes anywhere until I say so. Risa, if you can hear me, wave your hand behind your back."

He looked around the corner to see Risa flipping him the bird behind her back. He smiled. Damn, she was bullheaded and brave. And he loved her. They would get through this.

He looked at head of hotel security. "Comments or suggestions?"

The older man shook his head. "Whoever this is, he doesn't expect to leave here alive, otherwise he wouldn't have used that boardroom. End of a hall. Only one exit. Nope, he's chosen the hill he wants to die on."

"My thoughts exactly. Suicide by cop."

"Or SEAL," the other man said.

Trevor nodded.

"Okay, Risa. Just do what I say, and let's go home. Get him into the hall."

Risa's heart pounded painfully inside her chest. Her hands had a visible tremor. She lifted her head and called out again, "I'm here. What do you want?"

"He said he's changed his mind," her sister said, her voice thinner than her usual brash tones. "He says you need to come in here."

"No way," Trevor said in her ear. "He comes out, or you're leaving. And don't argue with me that you aren't leaving. Convince him."

Risa drew a deep breath to calm her nerves. "No,

sorry, Wendy. I'm not coming in there. I'm in the hall, just as he asked, and I'm alone."

"He wants to know where your date is."

Risa drew another breath. "I left him upstairs. I told him I was going to talk to the mayor, and he believed me. Now, I'm here. Either come out and face me, or I'm leaving."

The door to the boardroom opened slowly, and Risa moved back. Wendy's face appeared in the crack. Her makeup was smeared, and Risa could see she'd been crying.

"I'm sorry, Risa," Wendy said. "I—"

"Shut up," came a male voice behind her. "Take two steps forward."

Wendy stepped into the hall with a hairy arm wrapped around her neck.

"Wendy. You okay?" Risa asked.

"Yeah. I'm—"

"Shut up," the man said, tapping the barrel of a gun against Wendy's head. He pushed Wendy a little further into the hall until Risa could see his face.

Her heart sank, and cold dread settled in her belly. Risa held out her arms. "I'm here, Mr. Compton. Nobody's been hurt. Let Wendy go, and you and I can talk."

"Like hell," Trevor said into her ear.

Ignoring Trevor, Risa lowered her arms. "There's no reason to hold Wendy hostage. I'm here. What do you want?"

"You know what I want," he said, spittle flying from his mouth. "I want my family back. I want my precious Rhonda back." He waved the gun in Risa's direction. "You ruined my life. You killed my wife."

"Mr. Compton, put the gun down, and we can talk. I'm sorry about your wife. I did everything—"

"Bullshit," he yelled. "If I'd had money, you'd have cured her. You let her die because I couldn't pay you for the drugs only rich people get."

"You can't reason with him, honey," Trevor said into her ear. "Step a little to your left."

"I am so very sorry about your wife, but I did everything I could for her." She moved a couple of inches to her left as though nervous, which of course, she was. Given how bad her knees were shaking, she was surprised she was standing, much less able to follow directions.

Mr. Compton's face crumpled. "My sweet Rhonda was my reason for living. Without her, I have nothing."

"You have your children, Mr. Compton. They need you."

He shook his head, his long, greasy hair coming loose from the ponytail at his neck. "My kids don't need me. I'm no good without Rhonda."

As soon as she'd seen him, she'd realized he'd been the man following her the day she'd gone into Manfrey's to pick up the necklace. He'd changed in the year since his wife died. He'd been a clean-cut salesman back then. Now, he looked as though he hadn't bathed in weeks. The stench from his clothing wafted toward her. It took all her acting skills to not flinch at the smell.

"I can't bring your wife back, but let me help you."

Risa took a step toward him, her hand extended.

"Stop right there," Compton said.

Risa froze. "Okay. Then why are we here? Now. Tonight."

"I've seen you on television, promising to help people like my Rhonda. Lying and taking their money. The only way you'll understand what you've done to me and hundreds of others is for you to feel what I'm feeling." His lips lifted in a sneer. "I'm going to kill the one person you love most in the world, and you're going to watch. Watch her life fade away just like I had to watch my Rhonda's life fade, because you didn't care. You didn't save her."

"Step left," Trevor said in her ear. "Now."

Risa scooted to her left.

"I said don't move," Compton shouted.

"I can't help it," Risa said, wringing her hands for extra effect. "I'm nervous, and when I'm nervous, I rock back and forth." She demonstrated by moving a little more to her left. When she did, Compton jerked Wendy around so that both he and Wendy were still in front of Risa.

"Trust me, sweetheart," Trevor said. "Drop to the floor when I say 'go.' If you understand me, say something to Wendy now."

"Wendy, I love you," Risa said.

"Now," Trevor said. "Go."

Risa fell to the floor like a puppet whose strings were cut. At the same time, a loud blast from a gun echoed in the hall. Wendy dropped to the floor in a heap.

Chapter Nine

❦

T*he Wee Hours of Sunday Morning*
Risa took a sip of hot coffee and shivered, not from any cold temperature but from the adrenaline still filling her cells. She glanced at Wendy beside her, and the tears flowed again.

"You've got to stop crying." Wendy draped her arm around Risa. "I'm okay."

"I almost got you killed."

"Not your fault." Wendy hugged her.

"I knew Mr. Compton was falling apart. I completely underestimated how far unstrung he'd become."

"No one else did either. Not his parents, nor his in-laws. I'm sorry that he died. His poor children."

Risa leaned into Wendy. "I don't know what I'd do without you."

Wendy squeezed her sister's shoulder. "I'll always be a pain in your ass. Trust me."

Risa chuckled softly.

Trevor joined them in the living room, stowing his phone inside his pocket. "We'll need to go down to the police station on Monday and sign our statements, but it's a closed case."

He sat beside Risa, who turned toward him and slugged his arm. "I can't believe you shot him with Wendy standing right there. You could have hit her."

"I didn't."

"But you could have."

"I told you to trust me, babe," he said, one corner of his mouth lifting. "I'm good."

Risa growled and lifted her coffee back to her mouth.

"Look at tonight this way," Wendy said with a wide smile. "The Breast Cancer Gala raised more money this year than in the last two years combined."

Risa's shoulders relaxed. "Isn't that wonderful? Think of all the women we can help."

"So, what's next for you?" Wendy asked Trevor.

He hugged Risa to his side. "I'm seeing all the Dallas Cowboy games with my dad and my brother in a fancy box next season." He kissed Risa. "Thank you. Dad was beyond thrilled."

"Thank you for letting me do this for you…and your dad."

"Not that," Wendy said. "I mean, where are you going next? This case is over."

"We still have to get that damn necklace out of here and to the museum."

Risa fingered the pink stone. "You mean this one?"

she said, widening her eyes in innocence. "No rush. It's only worth a couple of thousand."

Trevor frowned. "What are you talking about?"

"You don't think I'm crazy enough to wear a necklace worth twenty or so million dollars, do you? This is a copy. The real one's in the vault at Manfrey's."

"What?" Trevor yelled. "Why didn't you tell me? I could have saved a fortune in manpower hours."

Risa gave him a beatific smile. "But you ended up needing them."

Wendy lifted the heavy necklace to study it. "How do you know this one is fake? It looks so real."

"Easy." Risa removed the necklace and handed it to Wendy. "Look at the pink stone closest to the clasp. See it?"

"Yep."

"In the real necklace, that stone is a white diamond. In the copy, it's a pink stone. Because that stone is fairly hidden by the clasp, it's not that noticeable."

Trevor rubbed his face. "I swear, clearing landmine fields is an easier job than understanding women."

Risa patted his arm, enjoying his consternation. "But less dangerous."

"I'm not sure."

Wendy stood and handed the necklace back to Risa. She lifted the buzzing cellphone from the end table. "Mom and Dad are on the way up. I'm going out to the hall to head them off and take them to my place. I think Trevor will melt if Mom keeps kissing him." Wendy leaned over and kissed Trevor's cheek. "I'm thinking you're going to be around for a while, right?"

Trevor glanced at Risa then back to Wendy. "Yeah."

Once they were alone, Risa snuggled into Trevor's side. "What a night."

He shook his head. "You were pretty awesome."

"So were you," she said softly. Now that the danger was past, she liked how solid and safe he felt against her.

"I know trusting me with your sister's life was hard for you."

"Not really." She looked up at him. "Don't you get it? I love you. You hold my heart in your hands. I trust you with everything."

He sighed. "Sometimes, I don't think I deserve you."

"You don't."

He chuckled.

"But you're stuck with me," she said, tilting her chin.

"Is that a threat?" he asked with a grin.

"I let you walk away fifteen years ago. I didn't fight for us then, but I'm older and smarter now. I hope you are, too."

"You know I'll always be uncomfortable with your money."

She frowned. "Yeah, but I don't understand. Why is it a problem for you?"

"Take this necklace." He lifted it. "Not only

couldn't I ever afford the original, paying a few thousand for a copy would stretch my budget. I want to be able to give you the world, but I don't need to since you can afford to get anything you want without me."

She shook her head and let out a breath. "Oh, Trevor. You're so wrong. Only you can give me what I want."

His eyebrows lowered a bit, and his expression went still. "And that is?"

"Your love. There isn't enough money in the world that could buy your love. You're so honest and true. If you were a man who could be bought, don't you think you would have taken my dad's offer to fund your college?"

He shook his head. "I couldn't do that."

"I know. I understand that now. I didn't then. Having him pay your tuition seemed like the answer or staying on scholarship and letting me pay for our dates." She shook her head. "You knew your worth back then even if neither of us understood that." She pulled her legs up and got on her knees beside him on the couch. "You're more valuable than every dollar I have in my trust fund. I love that you love me for me."

"I do love you, although you drive me crazy at times."

She smiled. "I know." She let her gaze drop to his chest. "Do you know when I knew that you loved me?"

"When?"

She raised her head to lock with his intense gaze. "When you left for the Navy. You told me you needed to find your way in the world. A man who could be influenced by my money wouldn't have joined the military, much less the SEALs." She chuckled softly. "I was so furious when I heard about the SEALs. I couldn't think. I couldn't eat. I couldn't study. Even though I logically understood, emotionally, I was a wreck. I thought if I wrote you that letter and wrote you out of my life, I could move on." She rested her forehead against his. "I never moved on because there'll never be another man for me other than you."

He kissed her. "I would slay dragons for you," he said, his voice roughening.

"You did." She kissed him back.

"One question."

"Shoot."

"Do I get to pick out your engagement ring?"

She smiled. "If you insist. Is that a proposal?"

He kissed her, this time deeply, holding her tightly to his chest. "No. That wasn't a proposal."

He released her and slid to the floor on one knee. "This is." He took her hand. "I love you, Risa McCool. I want to spend the rest of my life loving you. Will you marry me?"

His eyes were so serious. His mouth, his beautiful mouth, pulled into a nervous straight line as he waited for her answer.

"I will if you'll give me something else I cannot buy."

He rolled his eyes. "You have my love, what else do you want?"

She laid her hand on her abdomen. "I want your baby, our baby."

"Oh, darling, I'll give you a dozen children if that's what you want."

She wrinkled her nose. "We'll start with one."

He smiled. "I hope it's a girl, and that she's just as stubborn and wonderful as her mom."

She laughed and threw herself into his arms. Happiness flowed through her, warming her all the way to her toes. They'd taken years to come full circle, and oh, the wait was worth it.

Trevor stood and hugged her, then turned slowly in a circle as they both laughed.

All the money in her trust fund could never equal the worth of this moment. The love of one good, honest man gave her riches beyond measure.

Note From the Author

Thank you for reading Hot SEAL, Black Coffee. I appreciate my readers. Without you, I wouldn't be here.

Readers are always asking: What can I do to help you?

My answer is always the same: PLEASE give me an honest review. Every review helps.

Cynthia

 New York Times and USA Today Bestselling Author Cynthia D'Alba was born and raised in a small Arkansas town. After being gone for a number of years, she's thrilled to be making her home back in Arkansas living on the banks of an eight-thousand acre lake.

When she's not reading or writing or plotting, she's doorman for her spoiled border collie, cook, house-keeper and chief bottle washer for her husband and slave to a noisy, messy parrot. She loves to chat online with friends and fans.

Send snail mail to: Cynthia D'Alba PO Box 2116 Hot Springs, AR 71914

Or better yet! She would for you to take her news-letter. She promises not to spam you, not to fill your inbox with advertising, and not to sell your name and email address to anyone. Check her website for a link to her newsletter.

www.cynthiadalba.com
cynthiadalba@gmail.com

facebook.com/cynthiadalba

twitter.com/cynthiadalba

bookbub.com/profile/cynthia-d-alba

Also by Cynthia D'Alba

Snowy Montana Nights

Carmichael Triplets Trilogy (coming soon)

Hot Assets

Hot Ex

Hot Briefs

SEALs in Paradise

Hot SEAL, Alaskan Nights

Hot SEAL, Confirmed Bachelor

Hot SEAL, Secret Service (novella)

Hot SEAL, Sweet & Spicy

Hot SEAL, Labor Day

Mason Security

Her Bodyguard

His Bodyguard

SEALs in Paradise Editions

SEALs in Paradise: Favorite Drink Edition
Hot SEAL, Black Coffee, Cynthia D'Alba
Hot SEAL, Cold Beer, Cynthia D'Alba
Hot SEAL, S*x on the Beach, Delilah Devlin
Hot SEAL, Salty Dog, Elle James
Hot SEAL, Red Wine, Becca Jameson
Hot SEAL, Dirty Martini, Cat Johnson
Hot SEAL, Bourbon Neat, Parker Kincade
Hot SEAL, Single Malt, Kris Michaels
Hot SEAL, Rusty Nail, Teresa Reasor

SEALs in Paradise: Vacation/Relocation Edition
Hot SEAL, Alaskan Nights, Cynthia D'Alba
Hot SEAL, New Orleans Night, Delilah Devlin
Hot SEAL, Hawaiian Nights, Elle James
Hot SEAL, Australian Nights, Becca Jameson
Hot SEAL, Tijuana Nights, Cat Johnson

Hot SEAL, Vegas Nights, Parker Kincade
Hot SEAL, Savannah Nights, Kris Michaels
Hot SEAL, Roman Nights, Teresa Reasor

SEALs in Paradise: Wedding Edition
Hot SEAL, Bachelor Party, Elle James
Hot SEAL, Decoy Bride, Delilah Devlin
Hot SEAL, Runaway Bride, Cat Johnson
Hot SEAL, Cold Feet, Becca Jameson
Hot SEAL, Best Man, Parker Kincade
Hot SEAL, Confirmed Bachelor, Cynthia D'Alba
Hot SEAL, Taking The Plunge, Teresa Reasor
Hot SEAL, Undercover Groom, Maryann Jordan

SEALs in Paradise: Holiday Edition
Hot SEAL, Heartbreaker, Cat Johnson
Hot SEAL, Charmed, Parker Kincade
Hot SEAL, April's Fool, Becca Jameson
Hot SEAL, In His Memory, Delilah Devlin
Hot SEAL, A Forever Dad, Maryanne Jordon
Hot SEAL, Independence Day, Elle James
Hot SEAL, Sweet & Spicy, Cynthia D'Alba
Hot SEAL, Labor Day, Cynthia D'Alba
Hot SEAL, Midnight Magic, Teresa Reasor
Hot SEAL, Sinful Harvest, Parker Kincade
Hot SEAL, Silent Knight, Kris Michaels

SEALs in Paradise: Song Edition
Hot SEAL, Under Pressure, Cat Johnson
HOT SEAL, Brown-Eyed Girl, Becca Jameson

Hot SEAL, Girl Crush, Cynthia D'Alba
Hot SEAL, Wild Thing, Delilah Devlin
Hot SEAL, Night Moves, Parker Kincade
Hot SEAL, Open Arms, Teresa Reasor

Read on for peeks at the other books in the crossocer
series
by
Cynthia D'Alba

Christmas in His Arms

Book TWO
Dallas Debutantes / McCool Family

My name is Opal Mae McCool. I love my parents, but
that name? Ugh, but I've adjusted. This year has been
rocking along until October when my entire life lands
in the toilet and someone flushes. First, my groom
dumps me at the altar. Confession…not as destroyed
as I should have been. Then, I share a steamy kiss with
old love which leads to…nothing. Radio silence. Fine.
Disappointed, but moving on. However, it's almost
Christmas and I make a quick overnight business trip
to Montana just in time for the snowmageddon and
I'm stuck in Bozeman with only clean panties and a
toothbrush. Next year has to be better, right?

I'm Michael Rockland. Born, raised and will die in
Texas and I'm fine with that. I'm a mechanic at heart,
even if my everyday job doesn't allow me under the

hood. About a month ago, I discovered I'm the Friday Lunch Special at a local diner. I'd be pissed if it wasn't for a good cause and it hadn't led me back to the love of my life. One hot, steamy kiss, a promise for the future, and she shuts me out. Harsh, but I'm a big boy. I can deal with reality, except when she ends up on my grandparents' doorstep in Montana.

My dad doesn't approve of him. His mother doesn't approve of me. It's not quite the Capulets and Montagues, and we are long past the teenage years, so isn't it time to let us decide if we belong together or not?

Snowy Montana Nights

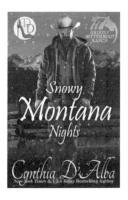

Book THREE
Dallas Debutantes / McCool Family

A cowboy who isn't what he appears must play
private host to a spoiled Dallas Debutante who
isn't what she seems. Between frozen pipes,
bonfires, bowling, a flu epidemic, a jealous ex-
girlfriend and a snowstorm of the century,
when will they ever find time to discover the
real person under their façade?

After an embarrassing disaster at her cousin's
wedding, Dr. Wendy McCool needs a change of scene
and some quiet time to reflect on her medical career
choices, her future and her lack of a love life…or
really, any life outside of eighty-hour work weeks. An
offer of a private apartment from her mother's friend

sends her off to Montana only to discover the unexpected.

After a decade in Chicago as a hedge fund manager and Zane Miller is ready to call it quits. He misses the family ranch in Montana, the fresh mountain air, and even the smell of a barn full of horses. When his mother falls ill, he heads to Montana, ready to do what it takes to get her health back, even running the ranch while his parents winter in Florida.

But he didn't agree to was playing host to a spoiled Dallas Debutante/jilted bride. Heaven help him.

Hot SEAL, Sweet & Spicy

Book FOUR in Crossover Series
A SEALs in Paradise/Grizzly Bitterroot Ranch

She's hankering for some happiness. He's facing his fate alone. Together, can they find forever on the menu?

Addison Treadway needs time to heal. With her love-less marriage finally demolished by her breast cancer diagnosis, the talk-show host never expected to also lose her job. And since her weekend as a bridesmaid is her last before chemo, the thirty-three-year-old resolves to put her perky girls to good use… and the groom's hunky brother is the perfect choice to kiss them goodbye.

Without orders to fulfill, Eli Miller feels aimless. With the former Navy SEAL's duties now turned towards the family farm, he's confused about what his future holds. And before he can figure out his next move, he finds the supposedly single woman he regretfully slept with at his brother's wedding is staying in his parents' apartment. Grateful to have acquaintances offer their home for her recovery from reconstructive surgery, Addison is floored when the sexy guy who ghosted her walks through the door. But when Eli uncovers the truth and sparks fly again, he starts cooking up something he's sure she's going to love.

Can they get past their awkward introduction and serve up a sizzling happily ever after?

Six Days and One Knight

Book FIVE
Dallas Debutantes / McCool Family-Grizzly Bitterroot Ranch Crossover

She thinks he's up to no good. He's desperate to catch her eye. When they're paired up for a snowy getaway, can they ring in happily ever after?

Brianna Treadway is thrilled to be her older sister's maid of honor. Except she has no date for the couple-centered ski vacation that's doubling as a weeklong wedding planning session. And when her sibling's high school ex is invited as her designated plus-one, she suspects he's coming along with ulterior motives to win back the bride.

Brody Knight is ready for something more. With his heart set on his best friend's younger sister, he jumps at the offer to head to the Montana slopes and charm the girl of his dreams. But he finds getting closer to the skittish woman is an uphill-yet-intoxicating challenge.

Determined to warn her handsome companion off from ruining the engagement, Brianna is mortified after slipping up with a secret confession. And as Brody works to convince her they're the ones meant for each other, he fears he's setting himself up for rejection that will leave him out in the cold.

Can they get a jump on the misunderstandings before they bomb past a forever love?

Made in United States
Troutdale, OR
01/04/2024

16695796R00096